Mia

the way the
cupcake
crumbles

SIMON SPOTLIGHT

An imprint of Simon & Schuster Children's Publishing Division

1230 Avenue of the Americas, New York, New York 10020

First Simon Spotlight paperback edition October 2015

Copyright © 2015 by Simon & Schuster, Inc.

All rights reserved, including the right of reproduction
in whole or in part in any form.

SIMON SPOTLIGHT and colophon are registered trademarks of
Simon & Schuster, Inc.

Text by Tracey West

Chapter header illustrations by Brittany Naundorff. Design by Laura Roode.

For information about special discounts for bulk purchases, please contact
Simon & Schuster Special Sales at 1-866-506-1949
or business@simonandschuster.com.

Manufactured in the United States of America 0915 OFF

2 4 6 8 10 9 7 5 3 1

ISBN 978-1-4814-4167-4 (pbk)

ISBN 978-1-4814-4168-1 (hc)

ISBN 978-1-4814-4169-8 (eBook)

Library of Congress Catalog Card Number 2015947031

CUPCAKE DIARIES

Mia

the **way** the

cupcake

crumbles

by coco simon

Simon Spotlight

New York   London   Toronto   Sydney   New Delhi

CHAPTER 1

I Told You I Hate Mondays!

It was one of those dreams that you wished would go on and on. I was at a fashion show, and there were tons of celebrities in the seats. And these models, who all looked like my friend Emma Taylor, were walking down the runway, wearing the most gorgeous clothes. And I had designed them all! Everyone kept clapping and clapping.

Then the dream crowd began to chant. *"Mia! Mia! Mia!"*

"Mia!"

I woke up with a start at the sound of Mom calling my name.

Why is she waking me up? I wondered groggily. She knows I set my alarm every night, and I wake up at six forty-five every morning—in time to get dressed, eat my breakfast, and, most important, do my hair.

I was feeling really cranky that Mom had interrupted my dream—and then I looked at the clock: 7:06.

"Mia, did you forget to set your alarm?" Mom called up to me.

I groaned in reply. Yes, I had, but I hated to admit it out loud.

"Mondays," I mumbled, climbing out of bed. Mondays are bad enough as it is, but they're even worse when you're running twenty minutes late.

I ran into the bathroom and quickly jumped in the shower. Normally, I like to leave my conditioner in my hair for a full three minutes, but I knew I didn't have time. I slopped it on and rinsed it out. It would have to do.

I toweled it dry and quickly got dressed in skinny jeans and a plain black T-shirt—classic, and my go-to look for when I'm in a hurry. And my black flats are the perfect touch.

"Mia! Breakfast!" Mom called again.

"I'll take it on the bus!" I called back down, and then I turned on my blow-dryer so I wouldn't have to hear Mom if she argued with me. I have this attachment that lets me comb and dry my hair at

2

the same time and makes my hair supershiny.

I had just finished the left side of my head when my blow-dryer made this funny wheezing noise. Then it just stopped.

"Come on!" I said, pushing the button in and out. I checked the cord and saw that it was plugged in. Frustrated, I pushed the button again, but it still didn't work.

I hated to admit defeat, but I knew it was broken. Now one side of my hair was perfectly flat, and the other side was starting to dry into a wavy mess.

I ran to the top of the stairs.

"Mom! Can I use your blow-dryer? Mine's broken, and my hair looks weird!" I called down.

Mom came to the bottom of the stairs and looked up at me.

"Mia, your bus will be here any minute. I made you eggs, and you are not going to miss breakfast just so you can make your hair look perfect. Please get down here right now."

"But I can't go out with my hair like this!" I wailed.

"Put it in a ponytail," Mom snapped, and walked away.

I was feeling pretty mad that she wouldn't let me use her blow-dryer, but I knew that the ponytail was a good solution. Or, at least, I thought so, until I tried pulling my hair into the elastic. The wavy side of my head kept puffing out, and it just didn't look right. I tried pulling it back again, and then I put it into a side ponytail, but that looked even worse, so I took it out.

"Mia! Now, please!" Mom sounded exasperated.

I sighed, slipped the elastic into my pocket, and opened my closet. My black flats should have been right there, in my shoe organizer, but they weren't. I checked under my bed and saw a lot of dust bunnies, but no flats.

Then I heard Mom coming up the stairs.

"Okay, okay!" I cried, heading her off before she could complain again. I grabbed the nearest shoes I could find—a pair of brown ankle boots—and ran downstairs.

"Finally," Mom said with a sigh when she saw me. Eddie, my stepdad, was leaning against the counter, drinking his coffee.

"Having a manic Monday, Mia?" he asked.

"Uh-huh," I mumbled. Eddie is really nice, but he is, like, always cheerful, and I just don't have that in me.

You'd think that my stepbrother, Dan, would be the same as Eddie, but he's really not. Dan is into this screaming metal kind of music and wears a lot of very uncheerful T-shirts with flaming skulls on them. He walks to the high school every morning, so he was already out the door when I got down.

I quickly ate my eggs and didn't even have time to brush my teeth before I had to go make the bus. Gross! I slipped on my brown boots, annoyed because they totally ruined the look of the sleek black T-shirt and skinny jeans. Then when I grabbed my backpack and ran for the door, Mom thrust an umbrella into my hand.

"You'll need this," she said.

"Why?" I asked, in a kind of haze, and then she opened the door for me and I saw that it was pouring rain outside. I mean, *pouring* rain.

"Bus, Mia," Mom said firmly.

Glaring at her, I opened the umbrella and stepped outside. Even the rain felt warm and gross, like dog drool.

I guess it was kind of good I was running late for the bus, because I didn't have to wait long for it to get there. I climbed on and slid down into my regular seat, feeling miserable.

At the next stop, my best friend, Katie Brown, got on and took the seat next to me, like she had ever since our first day at middle school (that's how we met). Katie usually cheers me up.

But not today.

"Hey, Mia," she said. Then she kind of stared at me. "Cool hairdo. Is that a new thing, half flat and half all wavy like that?"

I was immediately upset. Now, Katie wasn't being mean or sarcastic at all. She doesn't know anything about fashion, really, except what I tell her. She mostly wears regular jeans and T-shirts with flowers or cupcakes on them, and I don't think she even blow-dries her hair. Which is fine, because Katie is adorable and perfect the way she is.

The reason I was upset is because if *Katie* noticed my hair—Katie, who never pays attention to what anybody's wearing or what their hair looks like—then that meant that everyone else at school was definitely going to notice.

"What's wrong?" she asked. I must have been wearing my upsetness on my face.

I sighed and sank down farther into the seat. "Monday," I replied, and that was all Katie needed to hear. She nodded.

"Yeah, Monday," she said. And we didn't say another word until we got to school, because Katie totally gets me. Which is why she's my best friend.

When we got to school, the linoleum floor was slippery and wet from everyone bringing the rain in with them, and the hallway smelled like a big wet sock. I made my way to my locker, self-conscious in my unmatching brown boots and with my bad breath and crazy hair.

Nobody is staring at you. Nobody is staring, I told myself, but of course, I was wrong.

"Nice hair, Mia," someone behind me hissed. A mean giggle followed.

I didn't have to turn around to know who it was. It was Olivia Allen. We had been friends for a while, but it just didn't work out. Olivia is as much into fashion as I am.

I turned around, anyway, and gave her a quick smile and wave as she passed me in the hallway. That's one rule of mine I always try to follow: If somebody gets to me, I try not to show it.

But the morning just kept getting worse. After homeroom, I have math with Mr. Kazinski. He's tall and wears glasses, and he's one of those loud, fun teachers who make jokes. That definitely helps make math class bearable, but the downside of that is he expects a lot of class participation.

Katie and I sit next to each other in that class, in the middle, which means we're in a prime spot to be called on. Normally, I don't mind, because Mr. K. doesn't make you feel bad if you get a wrong answer, but today I was just not in the mood.

So when class started, I decided to pretend that I was invisible.

He can't see you, I told myself. *You're invisible. As invisible as the wind. As invisible as . . . glass. As invisible as . . .*

"Mia? Earth to Mia?"

The whole class was laughing, and I realized that Mr. K. must have called on me and I hadn't even heard him.

"Oh, yeah," I said.

"Mia, can you tell me how we can find the perimeter of this triangle?" he asked.

I stared at the triangle on the board. I *did* know how to do it, honestly, but everyone was still laughing and I just couldn't concentrate.

"Um . . . uh . . . ," I said.

"Come back to Earth, Mia, and I'll call on you again later," Mr. K. said. "All right, who can tell me how to find the perimeter of this triangle?"

Katie gave me a sympathetic look, and I shook my head. Being embarrassed in class is not a feeling I am used to. And I answered the next question correctly, but still . . .

"Earth to Mia," Ken Watanabe joked as the bell rang and I headed to my next class.

"Don't feel bad, Mia," Katie said. "Stuff like that happens all the time in Mr. K.'s class."

"I blame Monday!" I said, and then we waved as we headed down two different hallways.

My hall took me to English class with Ms. Harmeyer. I like English class a lot, and we're reading a really compelling book about a girl who lived during World War II. So I was looking forward to second period.

I was, that is, until I sat down, and my friend Nora, who sits next to me, said, "Mia, what's that on your arm?"

I looked at my right arm, which was covered in blue ink. There was a big blob of ink on the desk, but somehow I hadn't seen it when I came in. Somebody's pen must have busted open.

"Oh, great," I moaned. I raised my hand. "Ms. Harmeyer, can I go wash this off?"

She let me go to the girls' room, and I tried to wash it off, but you know how that goes. I couldn't get it off! I scrubbed and scrubbed with a paper towel, but I still had a huge purpley-blue stain on my arm. I must have been in there for a long time because Nora came in and said, "Ms. Harmeyer is wondering where you are."

I turned off the water. "I just can't get it off."

Now it was Nora's turn to give me a sympathetic look, and I reluctantly followed her back to class.

After English I have gym with Katie, Alexis Becker, and Emma—my three best friends. Besides being friends, we own a cupcake business together. Cupcakes helped us bond on the first day of middle school. Then we turned our love for cupcakes into something really awesome.

It's nice that we all have gym together, because it usually means I end up on a team with at least one of my friends. Today, Ms. Chen, our gym teacher, divided us into four teams to play basketball.

Now, I like basketball, and I'm kind of tall, and I'm pretty good at it. But on that Monday, it was like I had never played basketball before in my life! I couldn't make a single shot. The first time I threw the ball, it rolled around and around the rim like it was going to go in, and then it slipped off to the side! The second time, I hit the backboard in the perfect spot, but the ball nicked the rim on the way in and bounced out. And then the third time, Jacob Lobel slapped the ball away as it soared to the basket—and he's the shortest kid in our class!

Because of me, our team lost: 10–8.

"It's okay," Emma told me, seeing my sad face

as we walked back to the locker room. "Everybody has a bad game once in a while."

"It's more than a bad game—it's a bad day," I told her.

Emma frowned. "Poor Mia. But cheer up! Lunch is next. Maybe the second half of your day will be better."

"I sure hope so!" I said.

CHAPTER 2

A Pop What?

"Oh, Mia, you still look miserable!" Emma said as she and Alexis sat down at the lunch table with their trays.

Alexis looked at me.

"I noticed that in gym. You just don't seem like yourself. Did you do something different with your hair?" she asked.

"Yeah, it's a new hairstyle called 'My Blow-Dryer-Broke-and-It's-Raining-Out,'" I replied sarcastically.

"Did you try a ponytail?" Emma asked.

"I tried," I said. I took the elastic from my pocket and slipped my hair into a low ponytail. "See how it bulges out?"

Emma got up and stood behind me. "That's

because you're doing a low ponytail. You should try a messy one, like this."

She undid the elastic and pulled my hair loosely on top of my head before slipping the elastic on again.

"Mirror?" I asked, and Emma quickly grabbed one from her backpack and handed it to me.

I looked at my reflection. The messy ponytail looked pretty good. And all my hair was mixed up together, so you couldn't tell which was the flat stuff and which was the wavy stuff.

"Thanks, Emma," I said, feeling a little better. Then I opened up my lunch bag.

"Cupcake meeting today, right?" Katie asked as she munched on a P-B-and-J sandwich.

Alexis nodded. "After school, at Emma's house," she replied. "I have some new business to bring up."

"And I recorded last night's episode of *Extreme Cupcake Challenge*," Emma added. "I thought we could watch it for inspiration."

"Cool!" Katie cried. Of the four of us, she is the most cupcake crazy. "Mom and I went to a movie with Mr. Green last night and I forgot to DVR it."

Mr. Green is a math teacher in our school—and Katie's mom's boyfriend. It's definitely awkward for Katie, but I think she's getting used to it.

"Let's meet in front of the school after last bell," Alexis suggested.

We all agreed that sounded fine, and before we knew it, lunch was over.

With my new messy ponytail in place, I was feeling a little more confident. And now that lunch was over, everybody had bad breath, not just me (especially anyone who ate the onion meat loaf at lunch).

Maybe Emma is right, I thought hopefully. Maybe the second half of the day will be better!

Katie and I walked into social studies together. I sat in my seat and put on my glasses. I need to wear them to see things that are far away, like when I watch TV, or I'm in class and I need to see the board clearly. I hated the idea of glasses at first, but now I'm used to them. The pair I chose for my main pair is very stylish, with thin copper frames. Well, more like half-rimmed frames, with nothing at the tops of the lenses, so it almost looks like I'm not wearing glasses at all.

Our teacher, Mrs. Kratzer, walked in. She's petite and has short hair and round glasses, and she's one of those teachers you'd call "tough but fair"—you know, strict but nice at the same time.

When the bell rang, she gave us a big smile.

"Good afternoon, class!" she said. "Time for a pop quiz!"

Her words hit me like a truck. I couldn't help myself.

"You didn't tell us there was going to be a quiz today!" I blurted out.

Mrs. Kratzer just kept smiling. "That's why it's called a pop quiz, Mia," she said cheerfully. "As long as you've been keeping up with the reading assignments, you should be fine."

She was right—I would have been fine if I had kept up with the reading assignments. The problem was, the latest issue of *Teen Runway* had come out a few days ago, and I had been reading that instead of my social studies. (Yes, I know it's only a magazine, but it takes me a long time to get through it. I take notes, mark the important pages with tiny flags, and make sketches when I get inspired.)

I sighed for the one hundredth time that day as Mrs. Kratzer passed out the quizzes. Katie gave me a sympathetic look—her second one for the day— but there was nothing she could do to help me; it was my fault, and I was on my own. I would just have to do my best.

I looked down at the paper and groaned. We

were learning about the dynasties from Chinese history, and I had a hard time keeping everything straight in my head. Was paper invented during the Han dynasty or during the Qin dynasty? Honestly, I had no idea.

I made my best guesses—some of the stuff I remembered from class—and handed in my paper. I knew there was no way I would get a good grade on that quiz.

Can this day get any worse? I wondered, as I scribbled forlornly in my notebook.

The answer was: Yes! Definitely!

After school, I walked with Emma, Katie, and Alexis to Emma's house. Emma has three brothers— two older and one younger—and usually one of them is around whenever we meet at the Taylor house. Today it was Jake, Emma's little brother. He's a total cutie, with blond hair and blue eyes like Emma.

"Are you making cupcakes today?" he asked, running up to us when we entered the house.

"Not today," Emma said. "We're having a meeting, so we need some peace and quiet."

Jake frowned. "I wanted cupcakes," he said, and then he ran off.

We unloaded our backpacks and gathered

around Emma's kitchen table. She put out glasses and a pitcher of water, and Alexis put a spreadsheet with numbers on the table in front of her.

Each of us in the Cupcake Club has a different role. Katie is great at baking and coming up with new flavors. Emma is a great baker too. I'm really good at coming up with cupcake decorations and displays. And Alexis has the most business sense out of all of us. She does the accounting stuff and handles our bookings and schedules. She's super-organized!

"So I have some bad news," Alexis said as we were pouring ourselves glasses of water.

Of course, I thought. Did I expect good news on a day like today?

"Our profits were down five percent last month," Alexis went on. "Compared not only to the month before, but to the same time last year."

"Five percent doesn't sound like a lot," Katie said.

"Maybe not, but it's a sign that business might be slowing down," Alexis replied. "Last month, we were down two percent. So we're seeing a steady decline."

"What do we do?" Emma asked.

"Get some new business, right?" Katie asked.

Alexis nodded. "Right. I've got some ideas. We can do a new round of flyers. It would be great if we could brainstorm some new flavors or seasonal ideas to advertise."

"We should watch *Extreme Cupcake Challenge!*" Emma said. "I bet we'll get some great ideas."

We moved to Emma's living room to watch the show. Jake was playing with some toy trucks on the floor. Emma and Alexis sat on the smaller couch, and Katie and I took seats on the big blue one. I put on my glasses to watch the show while Emma scrolled through the DVR menu on her TV screen.

Then Katie nudged me, holding out her cell phone. "Check out this cupcake site I found. The decorations are amazing."

It's easier for me to see small things without my glasses on, so I took them off and placed them on the couch next to me. Then I took the phone from Katie and checked out the site. It was amazing. I was trying to enlarge a photo of a cupcake with thin, perfectly curled chocolate pieces on top when Jake ran up to the couch.

"Mia, want to see my truck?" he asked, hopping onto the seat next to me.

Crunch!

18

Jake's eyes got wide at the same time I got a sick feeling in my stomach.

"Uh-oh," Jake said, and he scooted over to reveal my glasses—my very broken glasses. The thin frames had snapped right in half.

Emma swept over and picked up Jake.

"Mia, I'm so sorry!" she said.

"It's my fault," I told her. "I shouldn't have put my glasses down there."

"No, it's my fault for showing you my phone," Katie said. "Then you wouldn't have taken off your glasses."

I would have smiled at Katie if I hadn't felt so miserable. She's so sweet.

"It's okay," I said. "I've got my backup at home."

Actually, I hadn't worn my backup pair in a while. When I bought them, I thought it would be fun to have a pair of fuchsia glasses. Yes, fuchsia—that deep, bright pink. I figured they would add a nice pop of color to my outfits. I wore them a few times, but I ended up thinking they made me look silly. My classic glasses blended in with my face. But my fuchsia glasses made a statement—a statement I wasn't sure I wanted to make anymore.

I tried to enjoy watching *Extreme Cupcake Challenge*, but everything was kind of blurry without my glasses, and I had to squint the whole time. Then I texted Eddie to come pick me up and bring me home. When I climbed into the car, all I could think about was going straight up to my room and climbing into bed. I didn't even want to eat dinner.

This was the worst. Day. Ever.

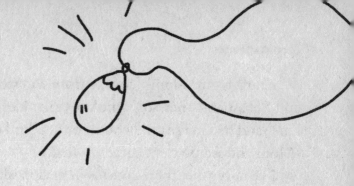

CHAPTER 3

I Need All the Help I Can Get

I was daydreaming about falling facedown into my bed when Eddie turned the corner of our street, and I noticed a bunch of cars parked outside our house.

"Eddie, what's going on?" I asked.

"Don't you remember?" he replied. "Laura and Sebastian flew in today. And all your relatives were excited to see them, so your mom invited them to our house to celebrate. Laura's house isn't ready for a party yet."

"Party?" I repeated, and my vision of my comfy bed quickly vanished. I knew Laura and Sebastian were supposed to be moving here soon, but I didn't know it was today. And I certainly didn't know there was going to be a party at my house on a Monday night!

Laura is my mom's cousin from Puerto Rico, and Sebastian is her son who's a year older than I am—and he's my second cousin or my third cousin. (Mom and Eddie can't agree on that.)

I've never met these cousins in person, although Mom Skypes a lot with Laura, so I've seen her face before. Laura has been saving to move to the States for a few years, and Eddie helped get her a job here in Maple Grove, at the company he works for. She's supposed to be an accounting wiz or something.

"So who exactly is here?" I asked Eddie, scanning the cars.

"Well, your grandma is here, and Aunt Marisa and Uncle Simone, and your mom's cousins Ian and Sofia, and a bunch of relatives even I haven't met yet," Eddie said. "Some of them took the train from Manhattan."

I quickly pulled down the sun visor in front of me and looked in the tiny mirror. My messy ponytail had only stayed cute for a couple of hours. Now it was weird and limp.

Perfect! I thought. *Nobody has seen me in ages, and this is how I look!*

"You look great, Mia," Eddie said, noticing me looking in the mirror. "Come on. Everybody's looking forward to seeing you."

I made an attempt to fluff up my ponytail, and then I got out of the car. Loud music blared from the house, and the smell of delicious food being cooked tickled my nose. My stomach rumbled.

The second I opened the door, a wall of noise hit me.

I heard cries of "Mia! She's here!" And then suddenly I was caught up in a tornado of hugging relatives. I didn't even recognize half the people who hugged me, so I was grateful when Uncle Simone pushed his way through the crowd.

"Let the girl breathe!" Uncle Simone joked.

"But I haven't seen her in ages," protested my aunt Marisa. (She and Uncle Simone are my mom's sister and brother.) She squeezed me tightly in another hug. Aunt Marisa is the short one in my mom's family, but she gives the strongest hugs ever.

Then she pulled back from me and looked me over. "Look at you! Gorgeous!"

"Thanks, but I'm kind of having a bad hair day," I said.

"Bah! You're fabulous," she said.

Seeing an opening, my grandma squeezed between us. She's the same size as Aunt Marisa and hugs just as hard.

"*Mija!* You're getting so tall!" she said.

23

"I missed you, Grandma," I said. "How'd you get here?" Grandma almost never comes to visit us in Maple Grove. We always travel to see her in the Bronx.

"Ernesto came to the apartment, and we took the train," she replied. "It's a nice ride. A lot of trees."

She nodded toward the dining room. "You should eat something, *mija*. I helped your mother make the rice and peas. I brought my own *sofrito* from home."

Sofrito is this mix of tomatoes, onions, garlic, and stuff that goes into a lot of dishes. Everyone in the family says my grandmother's is the best.

My mom walked up. She's taller than Aunt Marisa, but they both have the same dark hair and brown eyes, like mine.

"Nobody makes *sofrito* like you, *Mamí*," she said. "I don't know why I can't get mine to come out like yours."

"You just need more practice," Grandma said, and Mom made this face where she wrinkles her nose and makes this half-crooked frown.

I had to smile. My mom is the most stylish, confident woman I know. But when she's around Grandma, she reminds me of a nervous kid. It's kind of funny.

"Before Mia eats, I'd like her to meet Laura," Mom said. "They've never met."

"Good, yes, go meet Laura," Grandma said, giving me a little push.

Mom led me into the living room, where a woman with highlighted, wavy brown hair was sitting on the couch. My dogs, Tiki and Milkshake, were both vying for a position on her lap. That was a good sign, I thought. When they like somebody, that person is usually worth liking.

"Laura, this is Mia," Mom said.

"Mia! Come, sit," she said, patting the seat on the couch next to her. "Sorry I'm not standing, but I'm wiped out from the plane ride."

Laura has lived all her life in Puerto Rico, so she speaks with a Puerto Rican accent. But I've grown up listening to accents, so it's not a big deal for me.

"It's so nice to see you in person!" Laura said, reaching across the dogs to give my shoulder a squeeze.

"You, too," I said. Then I added automatically, "I'm having a bad hair day."

"Well, with this rain, who isn't?" Laura asked, and I really liked her answer. She wasn't pretending my hair looked great when I clearly knew that it didn't. "So how was your Cupcake meeting? That business is still going strong?"

I nodded. "Yes. Although my friend Alexis says our profits are down, so we're looking for new ideas."

"If you ever need accounting help, just let me know," Laura said. Then she squinted at me. "*Mija*, you have braces! I never saw those on Skype."

"They're the clear kind," I explained. "I got them the same time I found out I needed glasses."

Then I remembered—my glasses! Having to wear my fuchsia glasses wasn't the worst of it. I was going to have to tell my mom about the broken pair.

"What's wrong?" Laura asked, seeing my face.

"Bad day," I said. "I am having just the worst luck."

Laura nodded. "That can be a serious problem, *mija*," she said. "Wait, have you met Sebastian yet?"

I shook my head. "No, I was too busy getting crushed by aunts and uncles," I replied.

Laura scanned the living room. "I just saw him. . . . There he is!"

She pointed to a corner of the room, where Sebastian was leaning against the wall, talking to Dan. They're both in high school, but Dan is a senior, and Sebastian is a freshman. They're both the same height, but Sebastian is skinny. I noticed he seemed to have dyed his already dark hair pitch-black.

Sebastian and Dan seemed to be talking very seriously about something. At first I was wondering what they had to talk about, and then I realized they were both dressed alike, in jeans and T-shirts with logos of screaming metal bands on them.

They must like the same kind of music, I guessed.

"Sebastian! Come meet Mia!" Laura yelled across the room.

Sebastian rolled his eyes. "In a minute!"

"Sebastian!" Laura yelled again, and Sebastian sighed and walked over.

"This is your cousin Mia," Laura told him.

"Hey," I said.

Sebastian nodded. "Hey. Your stepbrother is cool."

"Um, yeah, sure," I said awkwardly. I had never thought of Dan as cool. Quiet, maybe. An expert at grunting one-word answers. A nice enough stepbrother. But cool?

"All right, so nice to see you," Sebastian said, and then he walked back to Dan.

Now Laura rolled her eyes. "It's like I never taught him manners," she said.

Then her stomach growled loudly, and instead of being embarrassed, she laughed. "Mia, how about getting your cousin a plate of food?" Laura asked.

"Sure thing," I said. "What do you want?"

"A little of everything would be good," she said. "I have a feeling I'm going to have to share it with these dogs."

"I can put them away if you want," I offered.

But she pulled them to her. "No, no, they're my friends!"

I laughed and then headed into the dining room. Mom had gone all fancy, and she'd put the good white tablecloth on the table, and there were those catering trays set up with Sternos under them. There was a big tray of chicken, and a tray of rice and peas, and one of broccoli and carrots (Mom is a big vegetable fan), and a tray of baked ziti, and at the end was a big cold tray of salad and bread.

I filled a plate with one of everything, and it looked so good that I decided to make a plate for myself, too. I picked up two plastic forks and napkins and carried them, along with the two plates, back to the living room.

I was halfway across the room when Tiki and Milkshake jumped off Laura's lap and came to greet me. I dodged a little to avoid them—and both plates flipped over in my hands! The food spilled onto the living room carpet.

I stood, stunned, frozen in place. A cry went up around the room, and Tiki and Milkshake started eating everything, and it was all so much that I could feel the tears forming in my eyes.

Eddie swept in with paper towels. "Not a big deal, Mia. We'll get this cleaned up."

"I'll help," I said, running into the kitchen.

But the army of aunt and uncles and cousins had already poured in, spraying the rug with carpet cleaner, and by the time I came back with more paper towels, there was no sign of the food on the carpet at all. And Laura was on the couch, happily eating a plate of food.

"Mia, come here," she said. "There's a plate for you too."

I sat next to her. "Thanks. I don't know if I feel like eating, though. With all the bad luck I'm having, I'll probably choke or have an allergic reaction or something."

Laura put down her fork. "Tell me about this bad luck."

"It just won't stop!" I said, glad to have someone who would listen. "I slept late, and my blow-dryer broke, and there was a pop quiz, and the cupcake business is bad, and I broke my glasses. . . ."

Laura held up a hand. "Do not say another word. I have just the thing for you."

She picked up her purse from the floor and started rummaging through it. She pulled out something, palm closed.

"Hold out your hand," she instructed.

Curious, I did as I was told. She placed something upon it: a silver chain with a black stone hanging from it.

"I want you to have my *azabache*," she said.

"*Azabache*?" I repeated.

"The stone. We give them to babies to protect them when they are born. This was mine. I carry it around to bring me luck. But I have very good luck, moving here," she said. "Now you need the good luck."

I looked at the little black stone. Some people might say that believing a stone could give you luck was superstitious. But I didn't feel that way. Laura had been given this when she was a baby. That made it special. And besides, I needed all the good luck I could get!

"Are you sure you want to give it up?" I asked.

Laura nodded. "It's time," she said. "And, anyway,

I have other good luck charms. After all, you can't have too much good luck!"

I hugged her. "Thank you. I will take good care of it."

Laura helped me attach the bracelet to my right wrist, and I focused on the stone as it dangled. I hoped Laura was right about the *azabache*. I couldn't take another day like this miserable Monday!

CHAPTER 4

Tuesday Turnaround

Oooh, yeah, yeah, yeah . . .

Tuesday morning I woke up to the tuneful sound of a song playing on my clock radio. The time glowed 6:45. Perfect!

Sitting up, the first thing I noticed was that I did not hear the pounding of the rain on the roof anymore. I went to the window and pulled aside the curtain. The morning sun was just rising, but I could see its first rays. It looked like it was going to be a sunny day.

I took my shower and let the conditioner stay in my hair for a full three minutes. When I got out, I panicked for a second—I still had a broken blow dryer!

Turns out, I didn't. There was a note on my blow-dryer on the dresser:

Fixed it! ☺ E.

So Eddie had fixed it for me. How and when, I don't know, because our relatives had stayed until pretty late and he had been busy helping Mom clean up the mess. But somehow he'd done it, and, boy, was I glad.

I dried my hair, using the straightening attachment, and with no humidity in the air, it came out perfect—straight and shiny.

Then I went to my closet to pick out an outfit, and I hesitated. I would be wearing those fuchsia glasses in every class. What could I wear that wouldn't draw too much attention to them?

Black again, I decided. My black button-down collared shirt, and maybe a denim skirt. If only I could find my black flats . . .

And suddenly, there they were! Right there in my shoe organizer where I had left them! But why hadn't I seen them yesterday?

I looked down at the *azabache* dangling from my wrist. I had slept with the bracelet on all night. Could that be the reason my luck was changing?

Maybe, but not everything was going to work

out my way today. I still hadn't told Mom about my glasses—and I knew I had to. So even though my reflection told me I looked fabulous—from my perfect hair down to my black flats—I didn't bound down the stairs like a baby deer or anything. More like I sort of plodded down like a turtle.

"Morning, Mia," Mom said. "Nice to see you on time today."

Then she looked at me closely. "What's wrong? You look like something's bothering you."

I took a deep breath. "I broke my glasses yesterday," I said, just getting it right out there. "It was an accident. I put them down on Emma's couch for just a second, and Jake jumped on them."

"Oh no," Mom said. "How bad?"

I fished them out of my backpack and handed the pieces to her. "Bad," I told her.

Mom examined them. "Well, they can't be fixed. But I think your service agreement is still good, and I might be able to get you a new pair for no charge."

"Really?" I asked.

"I'll call today," Mom said. "Do you have your backup glasses?"

I slipped them out of my skirt pocket and put

them on. "Yup. Fun fuchsia. Can you believe I ever picked these out?"

"But they're cute!" Mom said. "Very young and fun. I know at least three clients who would love a pair of those."

Mom is a fashion stylist—which is probably why I am so into fashion. It's in my blood, and besides that, I grew up around fashion my whole life. When we lived in Manhattan, she sometimes styled celebrities. She still styles models for fashion shows, but now she mostly styles women in the New Jersey suburbs who want to look like celebrities and models.

And the fact that she's a professional means that usually when Mom tells me I look good, I know she means it. She's not just saying it because she's my mom. It would go against her nature to praise a bad look.

So in one swoop, two things I was worried about just disappeared. Mom wasn't angry about my broken glasses, and I could get away with wearing fuchsia glasses—for a while, anyway.

I held the *azabache* up to my face.

"Thank you," I whispered, and then I realized I was talking to a bracelet and felt embarrassed. Luckily, Mom had her back to me, Eddie was reading the newspaper, and Dan's face was hidden behind a cereal box.

I sat down to a plate of waffles (my favorite!) and had plenty of time to brush my teeth and give my hair one last brush before it was time to head to the bus. As I walked there, I noticed the leaves on the trees were just beginning to turn orange and yellow, and the air had that scent you only smell in fall. The new morning sky was a beautiful, bright blue.

This is going to be a great day, I thought.

I got on the bus, and after one stop, Katie was sitting next to me. The day before, I hadn't said a word, but now I had a lot to tell her.

"So I forgot to mention that my cousins moved here from Puerto Rico," I said. "Laura, who's my mom's age, and Sebastian, her son. He's a freshman in high school."

"That's nice," Katie said. "What's Sebastian like?"

"I don't know him very well," I admitted. "But get this: He dyes his hair black, and I think he and Dan are now, like, best friends or something. They both like that screaming metal music Dan loves."

"Well, that's good, right?" Katie asked. "I mean, it must be hard to move to a new school from far away. But I guess you know that."

"Manhattan's not that far away, but I get what you mean," I said. "I never thought of that, actually. Anyway, a lot of kids in the high school are into that music, so I bet he'll make a lot of friends."

Katie started to giggle. "Maybe on his first day he'll sit with somebody at lunch who brings in a cupcake, and they'll form a Cupcake Club."

I laughed. "Can you imagine? Metal cupcakes. With black icing."

"And green pudding inside," Katie said. Then she talked in a deep, growly voice. "Eat our heavy metal cupcakes or else!"

By now I was cracking up, and I couldn't stop. It didn't help that Katie kept talking in the heavy metal cupcake voice the whole ride to school.

On the way to my locker, we passed Sophie and Lucy. They're best friends who are both nice, and friends with the Cupcake Club.

"Mia, love the skirt," Sophie said.

"Thanks!" I replied.

Then when I was getting my books for first period, Olivia passed by. Unlike yesterday, she stopped this time.

"My gosh, Mia, how did you get your hair so smooth?" she asked, and I could tell she was genuinely interested—she wasn't trying to insult me.

"It helps when it's not raining," I replied, and Olivia nodded.

"You can say that again," she said and then walked away.

There were no surprises in my morning classes (no pop quizzes!), and when I got to lunch, I found that somebody (probably Eddie) had turned yesterday's leftovers into a chicken and rice salad for me. Yum!

I was digging into lunch when Emma noticed my bracelet.

"That's so cute," she said, holding my wrist to get a better look at the stone. "I've never seen you wear this before."

"Oh, right, I got it last night," I said. First, I explained about the whole party for Laura and Sebastian. Then I launched into my bad luck stories. "So the last straw was when I dropped two plates of food onto the rug! But Laura was so nice about it. She gave this to me and said it would bring me good luck. She's had this since she was a baby. It's a Puerto Rican tradition."

"Cool," Katie said. "I found a four-leaf clover once, when I was little. I keep it pressed inside a book. I'm not sure if it's good luck or not, though. Maybe I need to take it out of the book to find out."

"Well, my mom saved the first tooth I lost, and she gave it to me when I found out the tooth fairy wasn't real," Emma said. "For some reason, I feel like it's a lucky charm. Like, if I have to take a test, I make sure I have it with me."

"You never told me that!" Alexis said accusingly.

Emma shrugged. "I never thought about it. Do you have any good luck charms?"

"Find a penny, pick it up, all day long you'll have good luck," Alexis quipped.

"No way," Emma said. "You *would* have a good luck charm that relates to money."

Alexis nodded. "I'm not superstitious, though— I swear. But when I was eight, my dad and I went to the store, and he got a penny in change, and he gave it to me. I remember being so thrilled. And then we were walking out of the store, and a display of oil cans came crashing down and it missed me by, like, an inch!"

"Get out!" I cried. "Really?"

Alexis nodded again. "Yup. I could've been crushed or something. So maybe the penny is lucky; maybe it's not. But I kept it ever since, because you never know."

"Exactly," I said. "You never know."

By now I was convinced the *azabache* was

working. The day was going great! And when I got to my locker before social studies, I saw something sparkle on the floor near my feet. A penny!

"Whoo!" I cried, not caring who heard me. How weird was that? Alexis was talking about a lucky penny, and here it was—a lucky penny of my very own.

You can't have too much good luck, Laura had said, so I picked up the penny and put it into my pocket.

I was in a pretty good mood after that—until the end of the day, when Katie and I were heading for the bus.

"I have so much math homework to do," Katie groaned as we waited in line.

Then it hit me. "Math!" I cried. "I left my stupid workbook in my locker."

I hesitated. I knew I had to go get it—but then I would miss the bus.

"Argh!" I cried. "I've got to go get it."

"How will you get home?" Katie asked.

"I don't know—I'll text Mom or something," I said as I ran off. My bad mood had returned in full force.

I got the book and ran back outside—and the bus was definitely gone. I was getting out my phone to text my mom when Sophie spotted me.

"Hey, Mia, did you miss your bus?" she asked. "We can give you a ride."

"Oh, that would be great," I said. "Let me just text my mom."

Missed bus. Getting ride home with Sophie. OK?

Fine. Thank Mrs. Baudin for me.

"I'm good. Mom says it's okay," I said. "Thanks so much." I slid into the backseat of the Baudins' car as Sophie got in the front.

"Mom, we're giving Mia a ride," Sophie informed her.

"No problem," said Mrs. Baudin. "Just remind me where you live."

I gave her my address as she pulled away. She immediately started talking. "This has been a crazy day," she told Sophie. "The planning committee for the fund-raiser is so far behind. We haven't even gotten the ad in the paper yet!"

Sophie craned her head around the seat. "Mom's in the Maple Grove Historical Society," she explained.

"Oh, we went there on a field trip when I was in the third grade," I said. "I mostly remember the photos of the women sewing clothes."

41

"The theme of the event is the textile and sewing industry in Maple Grove," Mrs. Baudin said. "There's going to be a lovely film shown. That's all set. But the menu! That's still a mess. I have no idea what to serve. Sandwiches? Soup? Dessert?"

"Um, Mom, Mia and her friends have a great cupcake business," Sophia told her.

In the rearview mirror, I could see Mrs. Baudin's eyes light up.

"Of course! I've heard of the Cupcake Club," she said. "You do themed cupcakes, don't you? Could you come up with custom cupcakes for us?"

"That's our specialty," I said. "We have a large menu of flavors you can choose from. And if the theme is sewing, we can do some great decorations to look like spools of thread or buttons. . . ."

"Yes, yes, yes!" Mrs. Baudin sounded thrilled. "That would be perfect. How can I book the order?"

I reached into my backpack and took out a business card, which I had because Alexis made sure we all carried them with us, all the time. "I have a business card I can give you."

"My, how professional," said Mrs. Baudin. "Please hand it to Sophie. I'll be sure to contact you."

42

"Thanks," I said. "We won't disappoint you."

Inside, I was feeling thrilled too. Just yesterday, Alexis had said we needed new business. Now we had new business!

Mrs. Baudin pulled up in front of my house.

"Thank you for the ride," I said as the car stopped in front of my house.

"Well, it sure was lucky that you missed your bus," Mrs. Baudin said. "You solved my problem."

Yes, it *was* lucky, I thought, looking down at my bracelet.

CHAPTER 5

A Sunday of Surprises

The very next weekend was a Dad Weekend. Ever since my parents got divorced, I spend one weekend with my mom and the next weekend with my dad in Manhattan. So I have Mom Weekends and Dad Weekends.

Mom Weekends always feel like normal weekdays, because I am used to living in Maple Grove now. It feels like home, even though Dad's not there and I miss him sometimes. It's complicated, I guess. But, anyway, on Mom Weekends, I do normal things like clean my room and watch movies with Mom and Eddie, and do Cupcake Club stuff, and have soccer practice during the season.

On Dad Weekends, I stay at his apartment in Manhattan—the place I *used* to call home. Now, it kind of feels like I'm visiting a hotel or something. My room there is always clean, because I'm hardly ever there to mess it up, and Dad has a cleaning lady who comes in and cleans the apartment, anyway. And even though I have to do normal things like homework, Dad and I usually end up doing special things together. Things you can't do in Maple Grove.

For example, every Friday night on a Dad Weekend, we go get sushi at Tokyo 16, the best sushi restaurant ever. There is no sushi restaurant in Maple Grove; the nearest one is in Stonebrook, and it still doesn't compare.

And Manhattan has amazing shops and museums and art galleries, too. And then there's Broadway. This weekend, the first after I got my *azabache*, Dad took my best Manhattan friend, Ava Monroe, and me to a Broadway musical.

It used to be confusing to have two best friends, but now it seems perfectly normal. Katie is my best friend in Maple Grove, and I see her all the time. Ava has been my best friend since I was a little girl, and I see her every time I have a Dad Weekend.

You would think that my two best friends would be alike, right? But mostly they're not, especially on the outside. Katie has long brown hair that is sometimes messy, and she mostly wears jeans, and sneakers that are sometimes stained with paint or decorating gel. Ava is petite with adorable short black hair, and she's superstylish. She's half Korean and half Scottish, and she looks like a mix of both.

Ava loves fashion and is not so interested in cupcakes or food; Katie is obsessed with cupcakes and food and could care less about fashion. So why do I like them both so much? Well, they're both funny. And nice. And they both get me.

Tonight, Ava slept over after we saw the Broadway show. We were on the floor in my room, looking at the program from the show, when Ava noticed my bracelet.

"What's that?" she asked.

I explained to her about the *azabache*, and she nodded.

"Laura sounds like my grandma—my Korean grandma," she said. "She freaks out if she sees a crow because she thinks they bring bad luck. And she says she had five kids because four is bad luck. And she always brings us this sticky rice candy, and she tells me to eat it for good luck before I take a test."

"Does it work?" I asked.

Ava shrugged. "I think so. I always got good grades on my tests after I ate the candy. But usually I get good grades on tests, anyway."

"Well, I had a *terrible* day last Monday," I said. "And as soon as Laura gave me the bracelet, everything changed."

"Then keep wearing it," Ava said. "You might as well if it works, right?"

"Right," I agreed.

The next morning was Sunday, so I didn't need an alarm to wake up. Ava and I both woke up at the same time to the smell of delicious warm bagels and hot cocoa that Dad got for us. They don't have great bagels in Maple Grove, either, so I love getting bagels when I'm at my Dad's.

"Rise and shine," Dad said, tapping on my door.

"Did you get cinnamon raisin?" I asked.

"Of course!" Dad said.

Yawning and still wearing our pj's, Ava and I went into the kitchen and ate the bagels. It was a nice, lazy morning, and when Dad announced it was time to get Ava home and head to the train station, I was only a little bit sad. I'm used to the back and forth by now.

We walked Ava home, and I hugged her when we got to her building.

"Good luck with your good luck," Ava said, and I smiled at her.

"Thanks!"

We left Ava, and I thought Dad and I were going to get on the subway to go to the train station, like we always do. But Dad made a right off Ava's street instead of a left.

"Dad, where are we going?" I asked.

Dad looked at me and smiled. "We're going to make a couple of stops this morning, *mija*."

"Where?" I asked, but Dad kept on smiling and wouldn't answer.

I was dying of curiosity, but I didn't have to wait long, because after a few blocks Dad stopped in front of an eyeglasses shop.

"New glasses?" I asked.

Dad nodded. "Mom says your lenses are fine. So you can buy new frames here, and then your shop back home will put them in for you."

I hugged him. "Thank you!" I cried. No more fuchsia! And this was a pretty fancy-looking eyeglasses shop, so I knew I would find some great frames.

And I did. Thirty minutes later, I came out holding a little bag with my new frames—black, smart-looking ones this time. The frames were thin, and the rounder shape really looked good with my face.

We started walking, and once again Dad made a wrong turn at the corner.

"Okay, I know you're going the wrong way," I told him.

Dad grinned. "One more stop."

Curious again, I followed him two more blocks. This time he stopped in front of a big pink box protruding from the wall of a building. A big sign on the top read: CUPCAKE VENDING MACHINE.

"Oh my gosh, Katie told me about this!" I said. "We didn't think it could be real. They just put it here, right?"

"It's only been here for a little while," Dad said. "I thought you'd like to see it. And maybe we can get some cupcakes for your club meeting this afternoon."

"Yes! I can't wait to try it!" I said, and I got in line. And yes, there were about five people in front of me to buy cupcakes.

I watched to see how the people in front of me did it. After you put your money in, a screen popped up. There were a dozen cupcakes to choose from! I had never even seen some of the flavors before. Pineapple ginger? Caramelized plum with cardamom? (I made a note to myself to ask Katie what the heck cardamom was.)

Finally, it was my turn, and Dad put a credit card into the machine.

"Do you want one?" I asked.

Dad patted his stomach. "No, thanks. That bagel is all the carbs I need today."

As I was waiting in line, I figured out what I wanted to get. I chose a range from basic to exotic. One black and white (vanilla cake with chocolate icing), one lemon coconut, one banana peanut butter. And I went for the cardamom one just because I was supercurious.

Each cupcake came out in its own perfect box. Dad, who thinks of everything, had brought a small shopping bag with handles. The boxes fit inside perfectly.

"Now you can carry them on the train without squishing them," he said.

I hugged him again. "You are the best! Thank you!"

Normally, on the train ride home, I draw in my sketchbook or do stuff on my phone. But today I just held the cupcake bag on my lap, looking out the window. I didn't feel bored; just peaceful, I guess. It had been a great weekend, and I felt really happy. I couldn't wait to show Katie those cupcakes!

Mom was there to pick me up at the Maple Grove train station, and I showed her my new frames. She promised to get the lenses fit into them in a day or two. When we pulled up to the house, I heard loud noises coming from inside.

"Another party?" I asked Mom.

"Well, not exactly," she replied as I opened the door. She had a funny look on her face.

The sound of loud music assaulted me. Eddie walked up to greet us.

"What's going on?" I asked Eddie.

"Missed you, Mia," Eddie said, giving me a hug. "That's Dan and Sebastian's band. They're using the basement to practice."

He had to practically shout over the music.

"Seriously?" I asked. "This is insane!"

"Yeah," Eddie said, with a slight shrug. "It's a little loud now. We're going to put some foam on the ceiling to cut down the sound."

I looked at Mom, and the look on her face told me everything. She didn't like it any more than I did, but she had gone along with it to keep the peace with Eddie.

"But I've got a Cupcake meeting soon," I protested.

"Don't worry," Eddie said. "I told them they

51

have to stop before your meeting starts. That's fair to everybody, right?" he asked, but he was smiling at Mom, his eyes like a hopeful puppy's.

"Can I please have some earplugs until this is over?" I shouted.

Mom and Eddie didn't answer, so I just gave a big sigh and put my bag away in my room. Then I set up the dining room for our meeting, putting the cupcake boxes in the middle of the table.

I didn't even hear the doorbell when it rang. I only knew my friends had arrived because Tiki and Milkshake suddenly started barking at the door. I went to answer it, passing Eddie.

"They're here! Please stop this racket!" I shouted.

Eddie nodded and darted downstairs. I opened the door to see Katie, Emma, and Alexis standing there.

"Is somebody being murdered in your basement?" Katie yelled, and the music stopped right in the middle of her question. We all laughed.

"That's Dan's band," I explained. "But they're done now, so we can have our meeting."

We went into the dining room, and Katie's eyes lit up when she saw the cupcake boxes. She gave me a push.

"The cupcake vending machine! No way!" she squealed.

"My dad took me," I explained.

Emma held up one of the boxes. "Caramelized plum with cardamom?"

"It's a spice," Katie said. "It kind of tastes like—"

Before she could finish, the sound of stomping feet interrupted her. Two of Dan's friends, wearing scary T-shirts, emerged from the basement and went out the front door without a word. We couldn't help staring at them. Then Dan and Sebastian came up.

"That was really good, dude," Dan said.

"Yeah," Sebastian said, nodding. Then he looked over at us. "Hi, Mia! Are these your friends?"

Dan walked up to his room without another word, but Sebastian strolled over to us and took a seat.

"Cupcakes? Is this a cupcake party?" he asked.

"It's a business meeting," I said. "We have a cupcake business."

Mom stuck her head into the dining room. "Sebastian, you're staying for dinner. Your mom is working late."

Sebastian smiled. *"Gracias."*

"Oh, you're Mia's cousin!" Katie cried. "Mia told us about you. I'm Katie."

"And this is Emma and Alexis," I said, feeling bad I had forgotten to introduce everyone.

"I'll get a knife from your mom so we can cut up the cupcakes and try them," Katie said. "I'll get plates, too. You want to try some, Sebastian?"

He nodded. "*Sí*, thank you."

I wasn't sure how I felt about my cousin being at my Cupcake Club meeting, but my friends didn't seem to mind.

"So, you're in a band with Dan?" Emma asked him with a big smile.

Sebastian nodded. "*Sí*, I play the drums."

"That was you? You sounded great," Emma complimented.

I wasn't sure if I was hearing right. That music sounded more like a truck crashing into a wall.

Katie came back in with a knife and five little plates. "You're a drummer? How do you hear yourself drumming over Dan's screaming? He sounds like he's seeing a ghost or something. *Aaaaah!*"

Everyone cracked up, including Sebastian, and I figured my friends were just being nice to my cousin and making him feel comfortable. Why else would Emma say she liked that music?

So we tasted the cupcakes, and then Sebastian went upstairs and we had our meeting. (Cardamom, by the way tastes lemony and a little spicy and gingery at the same time.)

It wasn't a superexciting meeting, but we went over what supplies we had and which ones we needed. Alexis and Katie reported on a small job they had done yesterday—two dozen cupcakes for a birthday party, and Alexis mentioned that Mrs. Baudin called about making cupcakes for her next week.

Then the doorbell rang, and Eddie answered it. A delicious smell filled the house.

"Pizza!" Katie cried.

Mom came into the dining room. "Are you girls just about done? I ordered some pizza for us."

"We're finished, Mrs. Valdes," Alexis announced, and if Alexis says we're done meeting, that means we're done meeting.

A few minutes later we were all sitting around the table—the Cupcake Club, Mom, Eddie, Dan, and Sebastian—eating pizza and laughing and talking. I munched on my veggie slice and got lost in thought for a minute.

Sunday had been full of surprises. New glasses, a cupcake machine, and now I had a screaming metal band practicing in my basement. Even with the band, it was still a pretty good day.

I was certain, absolutely certain, that my streak of bad luck was over for good.

CHAPTER 6

Everything Is Falling into Place

That Sunday night, I was getting my backpack ready for school the next day when I spotted my social studies book. I groaned. I had meant to catch up on my reading over the weekend, but Ava had slept over on Saturday. I could have done it on the train, but I'd totally forgotten.

I looked at the clock: 9:30. Not too late, but I was supertired from the long weekend.

Even if you read it now, you won't remember any of it, said that little voice inside me. My Impractical Mia voice.

But what if there's a pop quiz tomorrow? asked Practical Mia.

There won't be a pop quiz, Impractical Mia assured me.

How can we be sure? asked Practical Mia.

"Because I have my lucky charm," I said out loud. "I mean, charms." Besides my *azabache*, I had my lucky penny. I had put it on my dresser the day I'd found it. But it would be better to carry it around with me, I decided. I completely forgot about my social studies reading and instead looked through my fabric scraps until I found a small piece of dark-blue satin. Then I took out my sewing kit and hand-sewed a tiny little pouch for the penny.

I added a drawstring, which is pretty easy to do, and then I slipped the penny inside and pulled the string tightly. Then I put it in the front pocket of my backpack. Something about putting that penny in there, tucked away, made me feel safe.

Safe? Why had I thought that? I wondered. It wasn't like I ever felt unsafe. I hadn't been born in some prehistoric time when I was worried about being eaten by a saber-toothed tiger or if I would have enough food to last the winter. My biggest worries involved whether Mrs. Kratzer had a pop quiz in store or if Olivia was going to make a mean comment about my hair or what I was wearing.

Still, sometimes the halls of middle school felt like a jungle, and a comment from Olivia could sting as much as a bite from a deadly snake. (Not that I would ever show it.) So, yes, the penny made me feel safe, in a weird way.

I yawned. I was definitely too tired to do any reading, whether I wanted to or not. I got ready for bed, feeling confident there would be no pop quiz the next day.

But tomorrow is Monday, said another little voice inside my head: Worried Mia. *Nothing ever goes right on Mondays.*

That was before my good luck charms, I told Worried Mia, and then I fell asleep.

The next morning, I woke up an entire minute before the alarm went off. And I felt awake! Not wide-awake, but awake enough to turn off the alarm, get out of bed, and stretch.

I kept a checklist in my head as I got ready for school. Perfect hair? Check. Perfect outfit? Check. Bracelet on? Check.

Oh my gosh, I think I am becoming Alexis! Worried Mia joked. Alexis is the queen of checklists.

I could see why she liked them. When I left the house, I felt more confident than usual.

"You look extra nice today, Mia," Katie told me when she got on the bus.

"Thanks!" I said. "I have a feeling it's going to

be a good day, even though it's a . . . you know."

"Monday," Katie whispered. "The most dreaded of all the days of the week. Except that *Chef Showdown* is on every Monday night at eight."

"Is there any cooking show you don't watch?" I asked.

Katie thought about it. "Um, no. I don't think so."

I shook my head. "You should totally be on one of those shows one day. You'd be great!"

"Yeah, sometimes I imagine I'm on *Chef Showdown*, competing, and then I start to get nervous just thinking of all the pressure. And the cameras that are right in your face! I don't think I could do it," she said.

"Well, if you did do it, you would win," I told her. And I meant it. Katie is a great cook. She can make anything. She wants to go to cooking school after high school, and I want to study fashion design, so our plan is to both go to school in Manhattan. We could even be roommates!

So, I was thinking happy thoughts all morning. In my math class, I got every problem right on my worksheet. In English, we read a really interesting short story. And in gym, I made a basket when we played basketball. Finally!

At lunch, I was happy to see a pita stuffed with lettuce, tomatoes, turkey, and Swiss cheese in my lunch bag, along with carrot sticks and hummus. *Yum!*

"Thanks again for the pizza last night, Mia," Emma said as she dug into her cafeteria lunch of mystery chili.

"You're welcome," I said. "That was Mom's idea."

"It was nice meeting your cousin," Emma said.

"He's technically my second or third cousin or something," I said. "He seems nice. I don't know him that well, but he sure likes Dan."

"That music they play is crazy," Katie said. "It sounds like a dynamite factory exploding during a thunderstorm."

We all laughed—except for Emma. "I don't know. I kind of like it," she said. "It's different."

"Yeah, well, snakes and sharks are different too, but that's not a reason to like them," Katie joked.

"You know what I mean," said Emma. "All the music on the radio is like 'yeah, yeah, ooh, ooh, let's party.' It gets boring."

"Well, it's not about the lyrics—it's about the music," Alexis said. "I like to dance, and you can't dance to whatever Dan's band is playing."

"Actually, you can," I said. "Dan goes to concerts, and he dances in the mosh pit, where everybody just slams into one another. Once, he almost broke his nose!"

"Mosh pit," Katie repeated. "That sounds like an interesting cupcake flavor."

"Moshmallow," Emma said, giggling.

"Speaking of cupcakes, we never made any plans for that historical society job," Alexis pointed out. "It's coming up soon, and we don't have any ideas for flavors or decorations. Can we meet on Wednesday after school?"

We all checked the calendars on our phones.

"I'm free, but Mom is working late, so we can't do it at our house," said Katie.

"And our bathroom is being remodeled, so my house is out," said Alexis.

"I'm sure we could do it at my place again," I offered. "Although I'm not sure if Dan's band will be practicing. Although I think Eddie told me something about Tuesdays."

Alexis typed into her phone. "So Wednesday, at Mia's, after school," she said. "I'll ask my dad if he can drive us."

"I'll text Mom, but I'm sure it will be okay," I said, typing as I talked.

By the time I finished my last carrot, Mom had texted back.

Sure, that's fine. I think Dan's band is practicing on Tuesdays and Thursdays.

I gave the report to my friends, and everyone seemed satisfied. Then Emma said, "You have Ms. Harmeyer for English too, right?"

I nodded.

"I was thinking, do you want to work on that English project together?" she asked. "We could help each other out. Maybe tomorrow? I could come over."

That sounded fine with me. We had read this book about World War II, and Ms. Harmeyer had assigned this big project with a timeline about the war and stuff. It felt more like history than English, but Ms. Harmeyer says it's important to make "real-life connections" when we read.

Then I remembered that Dan's band was practicing. "It will be loud," I reminded her. "Should we do it at your house?"

"No, that's okay," Emma said. "Jake has a . . . a thing. I can be at your place at four."

I shrugged. "Sure." Emma and I had worked on school stuff together before, so I didn't think it was strange that she asked me to work on the report with her.

When lunch was over, Katie and I headed to social studies. This would be the test to see if my bad luck was finally over. Would there be a pop quiz or not?

But when we walked into class, a guy was sitting at Mrs. Kratzer's desk. On the board he had written his name: Mr. Cohen.

"Ms. Kratzer is getting a tooth pulled today, so I'll be your teacher," he announced. "She wants you to work on the timeline of Chinese dynasties."

I looked at Katie and raised my eyebrows. No Mrs. Kratzer meant no pop quiz! I felt bad about Mrs. Kratzer's tooth, but I was happy about not having a pop quiz. My lucky charms had done it again! And just because I had good luck didn't mean that Mrs. Kratzer had bad luck, right?

Of course not, said Practical Mia.

So I listened to Practical Mia and enjoyed my quizless class. Unfortunately, Practical Mia was nowhere around that night when I was about to open my social studies book and get my reading done.

Then Katie texted me. Chef Showdown on in 2 minutes! Watch it with me!

Homework 2 do, I texted back, but I was curious, so I turned on the TV.

You can watch TV and do your reading at the same time! said Impractical Mia.

And that was the plan, except I really got into the show—Katie was right; it was really good! And Katie kept texting me the whole time.

That looks delicious!
I wouldn't feed that to a cat!
Can you believe she said that?

Watching the show and texting with Katie was very entertaining, and I stopped reading my social studies book, even during the commercials.

When the show was over, Tired Mia took over, and I fell asleep without doing that reading. But my good luck charms would protect me, right?

What if they don't? asked Worried Mia, but I drifted off to sleep before I could answer.

CHAPTER 7

Emma's New Look?!

I shouldn't have worried, because the next day, Tuesday, Mrs. Kratzer was out again. I felt bad for her, but at the same time I was relieved—no pop quiz!

"I'll see you around four," Emma said to me as she passed me outside after the last bell rang.

"Okay, see you!" I called back as I waited in line for the bus with Katie.

This is a good time for me to talk about what Emma was wearing. I think Emma has a cute sense of style, although she likes pale pink a lot more than I do. She wears a skirt almost every day, even if it's cold out. Today, she had on a short white skirt, and a cute pale-pink top with lace on the edges of the sleeves. She wore white flats, and a pale pink headband held her long blond hair in place.

Matching pale-pink lip gloss shone on her lips.

That's the Emma I know. That's the Emma everyone knows. She wears soft colors, I think, because she has a supersweet personality and a big heart. So it fits her.

Anyway, before I would see Emma again at my house, it was time for another bus ride home. When I moved here from Manhattan, I was really worried that riding a school bus was going to be awful. In the city, I took a subway to school. Some people think riding on a crowded subway was awful, but that's what I was used to. For the most part, everybody keeps to themselves on the subway, and once you get used to the smell, it's not so bad.

That's what I was used to, so I was pretty nervous about having to take a bus to school when I moved to Maple Grove. Any time I had seen a school bus on TV or in the movies, kids were always yelling and screaming and throwing paper planes around and stuff. Luckily, my school bus turned out to be a lot calmer than that. And even when things got crazy, I always had Katie in the seat with me.

George Martinez and Ken Watanabe sit behind us, and they're pretty nice. Actually, Katie thinks George is *really* nice. If Katie's mom would let Katie have a boyfriend, George would be him.

Instead, they're more like an unofficial couple.

The members of the Cupcake Club all have had some history with boys. Alexis has a crush on Emma's older brother Matt, and there is some evidence that he likes her back. They have danced together at parties and stuff. And I'm pretty sure Emma had a crush on a boy at her summer camp, but I don't really know all the details of that. Frankly, we usually talk way more about cupcakes and teachers and stuff than we do about boys.

George stuck his head over the back of Katie's seat.

"Hey, Katie," he said. "How do you make a tissue dance?"

"I don't know," Katie replied. "How?"

"You put a little boogie in it!" George said, and then he started cracking up.

"Eww, gross!" Katie replied, punching the back of her seat, and George ducked back down. But Katie was cracking up too.

A teeny, tiny part of me felt jealous, but just a teeny, tiny part. I used to have an unofficial boyfriend, too—Chris Howard. But then things got complicated when I got busy with a fashion design contest, and Chris asked Talia Robinson to George's Halloween party. Now it looks like Talia and Chris are unofficial boyfriend and girlfriend.

Katie noticed my face. "You're still thinking about Chris, aren't you?" she asked.

"Not exactly," I replied. "I mean, the whole thing made me feel bad. But I don't need a boy-whatever in my life right now. I've got way too much stuff going on. Like Ms. Harmeyer's English project, for one thing."

"Yeah, thanks for asking me to come over and work on it with you," Katie said sarcastically. "I have Ms. Harmeyer too, you know."

"Oh, Katie, I'm so sorry!" I cried. "It's just—Emma asked me, and I totally forgot you had to do the same report. Do you want to come over?"

Katie grinned. "Actually, I finished mine already. Just wanted to make you feel guilty."

I shook my head. "Nice, Katie, nice," I said. "You and George are meant for each other!"

"Don't say that so loud!" she hissed, and then we both started laughing.

Then came Katie's stop, and it just was a short stretch to the next one—my stop. I could hear Dan's band practicing when I walked in the door.

Mom was walking out of the kitchen, holding a cup of coffee. She does a lot of her work at home.

"How can you stand this?" I shouted over the noise.

Mom took something out of her ear. "Earplugs," she said. "They drown out most of it."

"Did you get me any?" I asked.

Mom shook her head. "Sorry. But don't worry—they'll be done soon."

But they were still playing when Emma got there. (Once again, I only knew because the dogs went crazy.) When I opened the door, I couldn't believe my eyes.

Emma was wearing skinny jeans. Jeans! And one of the knees was ripped. She had black canvas sneakers on her feet, and she wore a black T-shirt with a crazy shark coming out of an ocean of flames on it.

And then there was her hair. The pale pink headband was gone, and she had added some kind of product to make her hair look messy instead of shiny and straight.

"Emma, what is this?" I asked. I didn't have to be specific. She knew what I meant.

Emma shrugged and blushed a little. "What's the big deal? Aren't you guys always telling me I should wear jeans? They're comfortable."

"But I mean . . ." I pointed to the shark shirt.

"Oh, that's Sam's," she replied. "It doesn't fit him, so he gave it to me."

"He *gave* it you?" I asked. "Why would he give *that* to you?"

"Because I asked him," Emma said, and there was a tone in her voice that told me I should back off. Which was not easy to do, because this was a major deal! Pretty-in-pink Emma wearing ripped jeans and a weird shirt, with messy hair? What the heck was going on?

But I took the hint and dropped it. "We can work in the dining room," I said.

Mom had already set up the table for us with some cut-up apples and a pitcher of water. I had put out some poster paper and my bin of art supplies—scissors, markers (thin and thick), colored pencils—I basically had everything we would need to make our timelines.

"Are you sure the music isn't bothering you?" I asked.

"I told you, I don't mind," Emma said. "Now, how were you going to do your timeline? Printing out pictures or drawing them?"

"I was thinking of sketching, but I think we can do a mix of both," I said. "Some of the images will be harder to draw, like pictures of military leaders and stuff like that."

So we got to work, and it was definitely much

easier doing it together. We were about a half hour into it when things suddenly got quiet.

"Practice must be over," I said. "That's weird. I kind of got used to the music."

Then we heard the sound of the guys stomping up the basement steps, and just like before, two guys quickly left out the front door, Dan went up to his room, and Sebastian came over to talk to us.

"Hi, Mia," he said. "And hi . . . I forget your name."

"It's Emma," she replied, and her cheeks turned pink—the only pink accessory she was wearing at the moment, in fact.

"Right, Emma. How could I forget a pretty name like that?" Sebastian asked, and he sat down across from us. "This does not look like a Cupcake meeting."

"No, it's an English project," I replied.

Sebastian made a face. "Homework."

Mom must have ears like a . . . some kind of animal with great hearing, because she popped into the dining room.

"Speaking of homework, Sebastian, your mom asked me to remind you to do yours," she said. "She's picking you up at eight so you have until then, okay?"

"Are you staying over for dinner again?" I asked.

Sebastian nodded. "Tomorrow, too. My mom's been working crazy hours at this new job. But she likes it, so . . ." He shrugged.

"Your practice sounded great," Emma piped up.

Sebastian smiled. "Really? Thank you. We still need a lot more practice, though."

Oh great, I thought.

"So you like our kind of music?" Sebastian asked. "Dan told me that Mia, you, and your friends like pop music."

"I like metal too," Emma said. "Have you heard As Glory Fades yet? They play them on the metal station."

Sebastian shook his head. "Are they good?"

"The bass player is amazing," Emma said.

For the second time that day, I was stunned. Emma and Sebastian might as well have been speaking a foreign language. Since when did Emma like screaming metal music?

I just watched them, dazed, as they talked about bands with weird names and Emma was nodding and laughing at everything Sebastian said.

Then it hit me.

Emma liked Sebastian. I mean, she *liked* him. She had a crush on him!

How did you not notice this sooner? asked Critical Mia.

Well, maybe because she only met him, like, once, and they have nothing in common, I answered myself.

Now that I had figured it out, I watched Emma and Sebastian carefully. Yes, she was definitely laughing too hard at his jokes. She *must* have a crush on him.

That made me wonder—did Sebastian like her back? He was a freshman in high school, which made him only about a year older than me and Emma, so that was cool. I knew that Lauren Reese in my Spanish class was dating a freshman, and nobody thought that was weird or anything.

So I studied Sebastian. He was smiling and stuff, but he's a smiley kind of boy, so it was hard to tell.

Then Sebastian stood up. "I should go do my own homework and let you finish yours. Nice talking with you, Emma."

"Yeah, you too," Emma said, and Sebastian went upstairs, I guess to do his homework in Dan's room. As soon as I heard Dan's door shut, I turned to Emma.

"You *like* him!" I said.

Emma blushed. "Yeah," she said. "It's weird. There's just something about him."

73

"So is that why you're dressed like that?" I asked.

"Well, partly yes and partly no," Emma said. "I mean, I really do like that music. Sam listens to it and I got into it, but I don't know anybody else who likes it. I never talked to Dan about it because he's a senior, but Sebastian is, like, our age. And I didn't think he'd take me seriously if I were wearing pink. You don't see a lot of metal fans wearing pink."

"Well, you look supercute, even if your T-shirt is oddly disturbing," I said. "So you should go for it! Mom has clients who pay her to give them a new look every year."

Emma looked down at her jeans. "This is definitely comfortable. But I don't know if I could dress like this to school. And I miss my pink!" She laughed. "Life is so complicated sometimes."

I nodded. "Yeah," I agreed.

Emma turned to me. "I can't tell if Sebastian likes me or not. Can you find out?"

"You mean like ask him?" I was a little startled. I'm not a fan of drama, especially relationship drama. Back in elementary school in Manhattan, there was always drama about who said what and who did what, but I didn't participate in any of that.

Then I looked at Emma's big blue eyes. She

really is a huge sweetheart, and one of my best friends. Saying no to her wouldn't be easy.

"Okay, I'll try to ask him," I sort of promised.

"Oh, thank you, Mia!" Emma cried, hugging me. Then she got a worried look. "It's not weird that I like your cousin, is it?"

I had to think about it. "Well, kind of weird," I said. "Like, what if you guys go out, and then you break up in some horrible fight, and then you don't want to ever see him again, but he's always here at my house? That would be majorly awkward."

"Not more awkward than Alexis liking my brother, Matt," Emma said. "And that's worked out fine so far. Seriously, I promise things would never be awkward between us. Friends first, right?"

I nodded. "Friends first."

That's always a good rule to follow.

Then you'd better hope that this whole Sebastian thing doesn't ruin your friendship with Emma, Worried Mia said.

It won't, I told myself, but I hoped I was right!

CHAPTER 8

Needles and Pins

After we'd finished the project and Emma had left, Eddie came home with a small box under his arm.

"Mia, this was outside," he said. "It's for you."

"My book!" I cried happily, and then I tore open the box.

One of the good things about the Cupcake Club is that Katie, Emma, Alexis, and I split the profits. That means I have spending money. Katie spends all hers on cookbooks and cooking supplies. Emma saved up to buy one of those expensive stand mixers (in pink, of course). And I don't think Alexis spends her money—I bet she's saved every penny.

I mostly spend mine on clothes, and fabric to make my own clothes. But this package didn't contain any of those things—it was a book on cupcake decorating.

It's not like I need ideas for cupcake decorations—I have lots of those. But sometimes I need help figuring out how to make my ideas edible and look good on a cupcake. For example, how about a cupcake with coconut icing that looks like snow, and a pine tree on top for winter? I loved that idea, and I knew the icing would look like snow, but the question was: How do you make a pine tree look like it's growing out of a cupcake? By piping icing? By sticking a tree-shape cookie in the top? Upside-down mini ice-cream cone covered in green frosting?

I tested all those ideas to see if they worked. The cookie was cute but a lot of extra work, and the cone looked awkward. When I tried the icing, I couldn't get it fluffy enough or stiff enough to make a tree that stood up on top of the cupcake. Then Katie found a recipe in one of her books, and when I tried it with the new icing, it came out perfect.

"You really need to get some cupcake decorating books of your own," Katie had told me. "After all, you are the chief decorator of a cupcake business."

"Yeah, I should," I had agreed, but I never got around to it. Then, when I had promised Sophie's mom that we could do cupcakes with a sewing theme, I realized once again I had ideas but not ways to execute them. So I quickly ordered a cupcake decorating book online.

And now our Cupcake meeting to plan the cupcakes for the historical society was tomorrow, and I needed some solid ideas to present to everyone. I couldn't wait to dig into the book. After dinner, I went right up to my room and started reading.

It was perfect! They had all kinds of tips for using fondant, which is a thick paste of sugar and water that you can mold or press into shapes. And in a section called "Cupcake Themes," there were four pages of sewing-themed cupcakes! I couldn't believe my luck.

Or could I? I looked down at my bracelet and smiled.

So I made lots of notes and did some sketches with color pencils for the meeting, and before I knew it I was yawning.

What about your social studies reading? Practical Mia prodded me.

I'll do it tomorrow on the bus, I promised myself, yawning. Besides, I got my English report finished, and that was a big deal, right? How much homework was a person supposed to do in one day, anyway?

❀

The next morning on the bus, I told Katie about my new book, and, of course, she had a million questions, and she recognized the author and had to tell me all about this other book the author had written that she knew I would love.

So once again—no reading! I was really sweating when I got to Mrs. Kratzer's class, waiting to see if she would spring a pop quiz on us.

"It's good to be back," Mrs. Kratzer announced when class started. "Let's review what you went over with Mr. Cohen these last two days."

I stopped sweating. No pop quiz! Everything was working out just great.

Now, I could have done my social studies reading after school, except I had a Cupcake Club meeting. Before Katie, Emma, and Alexis got there, I saw that Sebastian was over again, doing his homework at the dining room table this time and drinking a glass of milk.

"Hey, Mia," Sebastian said. "Your mom says you have a Cupcake Club meeting. Should I move?"

"No, that's okay. We can meet up in my room," I told him.

Then I remembered I was supposed to ask him if he liked Emma. Awkward! But I was saved by the bell—the doorbell. Katie lives just a few blocks away, so she got to my house first, as usual.

Katie grinned when she saw my cousin. "Oh no, Sebastian's here! I should have worn my ear protectors," she teased.

Sebastian laughed. "Are you criticizing my drumming?"

"No, it's great," Katie said. "It reminds me of the jackhammer that the guys fixing my street are using. I hear it every morning. It's better than birds singing."

Sebastian laughed again. "Come on. I do not sound like a jackhammer!"

"Well, kind of," Katie said. "But, anyway, you drum really fast, and that must be hard to do. Seriously."

He nodded. "I practice a lot."

"Yeah, I figured that," Katie said.

Then the doorbell rang again, and this time it was Emma and Alexis. Emma waved shyly at Sebastian, but he was looking down at his math book and didn't notice.

"So, I guess we can meet up in my room," I said, nodding to Sebastian. "He's doing his homework."

So we made our way up the stairs. When Mom and I first moved into the house with Eddie and

Dan, I wasn't crazy about my room. But Eddie helped me redo it. We painted the walls pale turquoise, and then we painted the old furniture—a dresser, desk, and night table—gleaming white with black trim so they all matched.

I wish I could say that I kept my room super-clean, but I don't. Mostly, there are clothes on the floor because sometimes I try on three or four outfits in the morning and just toss the rejects there. So I quickly kicked the stray clothes under the bed, and we sat on the floor on my turquoise rug. I have these big throw pillows—two black and two white—that are supercomfy and perfect for floor sitting.

Katie crossed her legs and closed her eyes. "Ohhhhhm," she said.

"Are you going to meditate during this meeting?" I asked. "Come on. That's not fair. I have a whole presentation and everything."

Katie opened her eyes. "Now I am at peace. We may begin."

Alexis laughed and shook her head. "Okay, so the event for the historical society is next week. The theme of the event is to celebrate the history of the textile and sewing industry in Maple Grove. Mia, do you have decoration ideas?"

I opened up my sketchbook and held it up so

everyone could see my designs. "So, I had been thinking that we could do really cute sewing decorations, like spools of thread, buttons, and balls of yarn."

Emma leaned in to look at my sketches, which I'd done with my color pencils. One cupcake had a tiny spool of blue thread and three buttons in happy yellow and pink colors. Another one had a red ball of yarn.

"That is so cute!" she said.

"Thanks," I said. "The problem was, I had no idea how to make them. So I ordered a cupcake decorating book, and I got some ideas."

I pointed to the buttons. "The buttons are easy. You just use real buttons almost like rubber stamps and press them into the fondant. Then you cut around the edges."

"That's genius!" Katie cried.

"The spool of thread is a little trickier," I explained. "You start with a sheet cake. Then you use a cutter in the shape of a tube to cut out the spool. Mini cookies make the top and bottom of the spool. For the thread, you pipe on frosting."

Alexis frowned. "That's pretty cool, but it sounds supercomplicated."

I nodded. "It is, definitely," I said. "But the results are amazing."

I held up the page in my book that had a color photo of the spools of thread. They looked adorable.

"Again, so cute!" said Emma. "We have to do these. It'll be fun."

"And impressive," Katie added. "That's the kind of thing people will talk about."

"Good point," agreed Alexis. "What about the ball of yarn?"

"We can make those out of skinny licorice ropes," I replied. "The only thing is, the colors are limited to black or red. We should probably stick to red."

"I love it," said Katie. "And I was thinking for flavors, we could do a maple cupcake. For Maple Grove, get it?"

"Perfect! I'll pass that by Mrs. Baudin," said Alexis. Then she frowned a little. "The only issue I see is that the cupcakes are due by five thirty on a Thursday night. It's not like we can spend all day working on them."

"How about, next Wednesday night we can bake and frost, and Thursday after school we can assemble the decorations?" I suggested. "We should have plenty of time. I'll get everything in advance. Besides, my luck has been great lately. We'll be fine."

"We don't need to be lucky—we need to be fast," Alexis pointed out. "And perfect."

"They *will* be perfect," I promised.

"Speaking of perfect," Katie said. "Emma, why is there a hole in your jeans? And now that I think about it, why are you wearing jeans? I thought you never wore them."

Emma blushed, and Alexis looked at her and raised her eyebrows, as if she were saying, *Tell her!* I figured Alexis knew all about Emma's crush, because Emma and Alexis are best friends.

"What's going on? Tell me!" Katie pleaded.

"Emma likes Sebastian!" Alexis blurted out, and Emma blushed again.

"Ohhhh," Katie said slowly. "I get it. So you're dressing like him now?"

"No," Emma insisted. "I like these clothes. And I like my other clothes, too. I don't see what the big deal is." She sounded a little hurt.

"I didn't mean it like that!" said Katie. "Sorry. It's not a big deal. But it's different. If I showed up wearing a pink dress with my hair all neat, I'm sure you'd ask me about it."

Emma smiled. "Oh my gosh, I can just picture that. You would look so cute! Do you want to borrow one of my dresses?"

"I would pay to see that," said Alexis. "And there aren't a lot of things I like paying for."

Katie quickly changed the subject. "So you like Sebastian? He's cute."

"Hey, what about George?" I asked.

"What about George?" Katie shot back. "All I said was that Sebastian was cute."

"He *is* cute," Emma said, blushing harder. "And we like the same music. I just never told you guys that."

"Then it looks like you two are a perfect match!" Katie concluded.

Emma sighed. "I don't think so. I'm not even sure if he likes me." She looked at me expectantly. "Did you ask him?"

I shook my head. "I haven't had a chance yet."

"I'm sure he does," Alexis said. "Who wouldn't like you?"

"Sebastian!" Emma wailed. "Mia, can you please ask him?"

"As soon as I can, I promise," I told Emma. Now there was more pressure than ever on me to perform this awkward task. And what if Sebastian didn't like her back? How would I break that news to Emma?

Luck, don't fail me now! I thought.

CHAPTER 9

Sebastian's Story

$\mathcal{M}$ ia! Why don't I hear you moving around up there?"

I slowly opened my eyes. Was that Mom calling me? Why hadn't my alarm gone off? I looked at my clock: 7:00. I was supposed to be up fifteen minutes ago!

"I'm awake!" I called out, and my voice sounded like a frog with a bad cold. I was far from awake, but I had to get moving.

As I quickly showered, I thought back to the night before. After dinner, I had done my homework and then sketched an idea for a new fall coat that had suddenly popped into my mind. Then I'd fallen asleep . . . without setting the alarm. I had been waking up without it for so long that maybe somewhere, deep in my mind, I had thought I didn't need it.

Then I had a scary thought. What if my bad luck was coming back? Then I remembered the day I had missed my bus, and it had turned into a good thing. So maybe me waking up late was supposed to happen, in a weird way. Maybe that would turn into a good thing too.

At least, that was what I hoped as I got ready for my morning. My blow-dryer didn't break, but I still had to pull my hair back into a ponytail because I didn't have time to make it look perfect.

Downstairs, Mom didn't bug me about being late, but I could tell she was annoyed.

"Just grab some cereal, Mia," Mom told me. "Eddie had to go in to work early, and I'm scrambling to meet a deadline for a client today."

I wasn't in the mood for cereal, so I put a piece of bread in the toaster and then went to find a sweater to wear with my red pleated skirt and white shirt, because I could tell it was chilly outside. (Oh, I forgot to mention—Mom had the lenses put into my new glasses, so I could wear colors again that didn't clash with my fuchsia frames.) I chose a black sweater, which was a pretty bold choice with the red and white, but with no time to spare, a bold move was my only option.

When I went to retrieve my toast, it was as black as my sweater. I mumbled complaints under my breath as I scraped the black stuff off into the sink and then buttered the toast. It did that thing when all the little black bits just stuck to the butter. It did not look very appetizing, but I was hungry, so I wolfed it down.

I barely had time to brush the burned toast off my teeth before I had to rush out to make the bus. I got to the stop just in time, puffing and panting.

I must have still looked sweaty or cranky or something when Katie got on the bus, because she raised her eyebrows when she saw me.

"Bad morning?" she asked.

"How can you tell?" I replied.

"Because you're not your usually smiley self," she explained.

I sighed. "It's not getting off to a great start. But I am not giving up hope. All this is happening for a reason. I just don't know what it is yet."

To my surprise, Katie frowned. "I don't like when people say things happen for a reason. Maybe some things do, but not everything. Like, I wouldn't say that to somebody who lost their house in a flood, or got really sick. That just doesn't seem fair. I think maybe sometimes bad things happen, and sometimes good things happen."

"Whoa, Katie, that is way too deep for this early in the morning," I teased, but I had an idea she might be on to something. But I was still cranky and sleepy, so I closed my eyes.

"Are you meditating?" Katie asked.

"No, sleeping!" I replied with a yawn.

I was still groggy when I got to school, and after homeroom when I went to open my locker, it was stuck! I had to ask Mr. Gregory, one of the janitors, to get it unstuck for me, and I was five minutes late to math class.

After math I had gym, and I was totally off my game. Not only did I not make a basket, I tripped over my shoelaces and almost fell flat on my face! At lunchtime, I was slightly disappointed to see that my lunch was ham and cheese on white bread—which meant that Mom made it, because Eddie always remembers that I don't like ham.

Where is your luck today? asked Worried Mia.

Hey, there's nothing unlucky about a ham sandwich, I told her. I'm lucky I have lunch!

Remembering that made me feel a little better,

until I got to Mrs. Kratzer's class. Things started off bad, and then got worse.

"Thanks to that darned tooth, I got behind on my grading," she told us when class started. "Here are your grades from your last pop quiz."

She passed out the papers to us, and there it was, right in my face: a D+! I am not usually the kind of student who gets failing grades. But there it was.

And that's when it got worse.

"Some of you had trouble with that last quiz, so today I'm giving you another pop quiz!" she said with a happy grin. "Since I know you've all kept up on your reading, it should give you a chance to improve your grade."

This time I didn't bother to complain. I knew that she was sending a message to all of us who hadn't done our reading (or was it just me?), but I deserved it. I had done everything possible to avoid doing my reading, and now my mistake was coming back to haunt me.

This is definitely bad luck! I thought, but Practical Mia had a different idea.

This isn't bad luck. This is your own fault, she reminded me, but I pushed that thought aside. It was much easier to blame bad luck than myself.

So Mrs. Kratzer passed out the quiz, which was

about more Chinese emperors who I hadn't read about, so I guessed a lot and hoped that my guesses would add up to more than a D+ this time. But I didn't have very high hopes about that.

I was relieved when class ended, but then my locker got stuck *again* and I had to ask the janitor for help—again.

"Not sure why it keeps getting stuck," he said. "Just one of those freak things, I guess. No explanation."

"Just bad luck," I said, and to my surprise, he nodded.

"Nothing worse than bad luck," he said. "That's why I always carry my lucky rabbit's foot." He jangled the key chain around his waist, and I saw a white, fluffy thing dangling there.

"Is this real?" I asked.

"No, they only make fake ones these days," he told me. "Otherwise, that would be pretty unlucky for the rabbit, wouldn't it?"

"Yeah, I guess so."

I was still thinking about bad luck when Katie and I got on the bus. I took my lucky penny out of the special pocket in my backpack.

"Does the luck in good luck charms run out?" I asked Katie.

Katie looked thoughtful. "Maybe," she said slowly. "But I guess you can't know for sure, can you? I mean, I think your lucky bracelet is special, because it came from your family. But maybe the luck in a penny doesn't last very long. We could look it up. Why?"

"Well, after I got the *azabache*, I had some really great days, all in a row," I said. "And then today, I woke up late because I forgot to set my alarm, and I burned my toast, and my locker got stuck twice, and Mrs. Kratzer gave us a pop quiz! Today was full of bad luck."

Katie looked thoughtful again. "It doesn't sound *so* bad. I mean, it sounds like a lot of normal stuff, right? Like, yesterday I slipped in a wet spot in the hallway, and I burned my tongue on soup, but I didn't think it was bad luck. It was just stuff that happened."

"I don't know. . . . That kind of sounds like bad luck to me," I said.

Katie shrugged. "I guess it's all how you look at it. You know, sometimes that's how the cupcake crumbles."

"Wait, isn't that what old people say? But I thought it was 'how the cookie crumbles'?" I asked.

"That's what Grandma Carole always says, but I changed 'cookie' to 'cupcake,'" Katie replied. "It's more fun that way. And, anyway, it just means that sometimes that's just how it is."

"I guess," I said. "You're right. Maybe today wasn't a bad luck day after all."

That's what I said out loud. But inside, I was still thinking about bad luck. After I got off the bus, I kept my eyes on the sidewalk, looking for another lucky penny, but I didn't find one.

When I got home, I went right up to my room and read my social studies book. The more I read, the more I realized how much I had gotten wrong on the quiz today. But I had to keep reading, and I got caught up by the time Mom called me downstairs for dinner.

Sebastian was setting the kitchen table for us.

"Are you living here now?" I asked him, half teasing. (The other half was seriously wondering about that. He was always hanging around!)

Eddie placed a platter of pork chops on the table and answered the question for Sebastian.

"Laura has been working late hours every night," he explained. "She joined us right in the middle of a huge project. But her schedule should get back to normal soon."

"She says she loves it," Sebastian told us. "I'm happy for her."

"That's a sweet thing to say," Mom said as she spooned green beans into a serving bowl.

Dan was making salad but not adding to the conversation.

"Can I help?" I asked.

"You can put the glasses out, please, Mia," Mom said.

In a few minutes we were all seated around the kitchen table, eating pork chops, green beans, mashed potatoes, salad, and applesauce.

"My favorite fall meal," Eddie said, heaping lots of everything onto his plate.

Sebastian was sitting next to me, and it reminded me that I needed to ask him about Emma. Asking him at dinner was kind of awkward, but I found a way around it.

"So, Sebastian, did you meet any, um, girls that you like here?" I asked.

"Actually, I have a girlfriend back in Puerto Rico," Sebastian said. "Or maybe I should say I *had* a girlfriend. She wanted us to break up when she found out I was moving here. But I keep hoping we can make it work. We talk every night on the computer."

"That's very romantic," Mom said.

Sebastian looked at me and grinned. "Why did

you ask me? Is there somebody you think I should like?" he asked.

Uh-oh. I wasn't sure how to handle that question now. It sounded like Sebastian was hung up on his girlfriend—or ex-girlfriend, whatever she was—back in Puerto Rico. If Emma knew that, she probably wouldn't want me to tell Sebastian that she liked him. Also, I had brought up the subject at the dinner table, which meant that *everybody* would know.

"Um, no," I said. "Just asking."

Dan put down his fork. "I bet it's Katie. It sounds like she totally busts you when she's around you, dude," he told Sebastian. "Girls do that when they like you."

"I said, it's nobody!" I insisted, but Sebastian was grinning like crazy, and I could feel my face getting red. My attempt at helping Emma was not working out at all!

"Who would have thought that pork chops would get everyone talking about romance?" Eddie said. "I've never thought of them as a romantic food."

"Then what is a romantic food?" Mom asked.

"Heart-shape pancakes?" I chimed in, glad that the subject had changed to food.

"No, I'm thinking maybe spaghetti," Eddie said.

Mom and I laughed. "But spaghetti is so messy!" I said.

"But it's Italian, and Italian food is romantic, right?" Eddie asked.

Mom kissed his cheek. "Any meal I eat with you is romantic," she said, and I groaned. Dan just kept shoveling mashed potatoes into his mouth. He ignores them when they get all gooey like this, but I still feel like it's my job to let them know when they're making me uncomfortable.

Sebastian seemed to understand. "So, what TV shows do you guys like to watch?" he asked, and Eddie immediately started talking about that show where people race around the world. I was relieved.

I would just tell Emma about Sebastian's girl-friend, and then I wouldn't be in the middle of this anymore.

It looked like my luck was turning around again!

CHAPTER 10

Just a Bump in the Road

After dinner was over, I helped clear the table. I piled all the plates and then . . . *crash!* The top one slipped off and smashed onto the floor, breaking into pieces.

"Everybody, stand back," Eddie instructed. "I'll get the broom!"

"I'm sorry!" I cried. "I keep dropping things lately!"

"That's because you're in your awkward stage," Mom told me as I stepped back to let Eddie sweep up the mess. "You'll grow out of it."

"Awkward? Really?" I asked. That sounded kind of insulting. "More like unlucky!"

Eddie cleaned up the broken plate, and as I finished helping to put stuff to away, I was thinking again about lucky charms. I still had my *azabache*. I had found a lucky penny, just like Alexis had, but that luck seemed to have run out.

I tried to remember what other good luck charms my friends had mentioned. Katie had found a four-leaf clover. I had no idea where to find one of those. And Emma had said that the first tooth that she'd lost was her good luck charm. Hmm.

"Mom, did you save any of my baby teeth?" I asked her.

Mom shuddered. "Why on Earth would I do that?"

"I don't know, maybe for sentimental reasons?" I suggested.

"And what's sentimental about teeth? I saved a lock of your hair every year until you were ten, though. I keep them pressed in a special book," she said.

Disappointed, I went back up to my room. I started looking around for something from my childhood that I could use as another good luck charm. I was digging around in my closet and got distracted by a pair of brown wedges that I had forgotten I owned when I spotted something: my first sewing kit.

Mom had given it to me when I was about five.

I'm not quite sure if I asked for it or if she was trying to encourage a love of sewing in me, but I do know that I fell in love with it. The kit came in a tiny wicker basket with a top quilted in pretty fabric that had little flowers on it. Inside was everything a beginning sewer needed: safety scissors with a pretty blue handle; a silver thimble; a pincushion shaped like a strawberry, with pins in it; and a little booklet that held sewing needles big enough for a five-year-old with limited motor skills.

I remember that I first began by sewing together simple shapes out of felt and then stuffing them. Then I started making stuffed felt animals, and then, as I got older, dolls' clothes. The sewing kit became filled with things I had gathered during my projects, like sew-on googly eyes for the stuffed animals, and scraps of fabric.

Sitting on the floor, I looked through the contents. A pin or a needle seemed like a bad choice to carry around as a good luck charm.

And then I spotted something—a pink button shaped like a flower. I remembered I had needed buttons for a dress for my doll, and Mom had taken me to a store in Manhattan that sold vintage buttons. I thought the pink flower buttons were the prettiest ones I had ever seen, and we bought six, all they had. I had only needed five for the dress, and I'd saved the extra one.

"It's perfect," I murmured, holding it up. I could even put string through it and hang it from my bracelet with the *azabache*! And that's what I did before I went to bed.

Finding the button also reminded me that I needed to get buttons for our next cupcake job. I needed to find cute buttons that we could press into the fondant for decoration. Vintage buttons like my pink flower would be perfect. But how would I find them? Maybe there was a store in Maple Grove that sold vintage buttons. Mom would know.

You should make a list, Practical Mia suggested, and I knew that was a good idea. But then I looked around at my room, which had shoes strewn all around it from my lucky charm search. By the time I cleaned up the mess, I was supertired and went right to sleep.

Before I knew it, Saturday came. My weekends in Manhattan with Dad always feel kind of rushed, because we're always going to and from somewhere. Weekends at Mom's are a lot more relaxed. On Saturday, I slept late, and when I came downstairs at ten, yawning, Mom reminded me, "Mia, do we need to go to the baking supply store today for anything?"

"Oh, yeah, we do," I said. "Can you take me?"

Mom nodded. "Get dressed and we'll go."

As I ate a bowl of oatmeal, I scribbled down a list on the paper Mom and Eddie use for shopping lists:

Fondant
Gel coloring for fondant
Tiny cookies for spools of thread
Skinny licorice for balls of yarn

"Mia, I have an appointment early this afternoon, so if we can leave soon, I'd appreciate it," Mom said.

"Yeah, sure," I said quickly, eating my last bite of oatmeal. Then I hurriedly showered and got dressed.

Mom took me to the baking supply shop first. I could spend all day in that place. It's filled with rows and rows of steel shelves filled with baking supplies. They've got decorating gels in dozens of different colors, and all kinds of molds to make shapes out of chocolate, and a whole row of cupcake holders and cupcake toppers.

But we learned early on that to make money, we have to spend money carefully, so I got enough fondant for what we needed and just three new colors of gel. Then Mom took me to Food City to find tiny cookies and skinny licorice. Luckily, we found both pretty easily.

"These cupcakes you're making are going to be adorable," Mom said.

"Thanks," I told her. "And thanks for taking me to get the stuff."

We went home, and Mom got ready for her appointment. Eddie was outside raking leaves, and I finished cleaning my room—actually cleaning it, not just shoving clothes under my bed. (Mom always looks there, so that might work with my friends' moms, but not with her.)

The day was pretty uneventful until the doorbell rang—and Emma was standing there in her jeans.

"Hey," she said. "Can I come in?"

"Sure," I said. "Um, Sebastian's not here."

Emma blushed. "That's not why I came. I mean, it would be nice if he were here. But Alexis told me that she booked three more cupcake jobs this morning, so we're in good shape. And I was out for a walk, so I thought I'd tell you."

"That's great news!" I said, and Emma followed

me into the kitchen. "I think Eddie made cookies last night. Want some?"

"Thanks," Emma said, and we sat down for some cookies and milk.

I took a deep breath. "So, I talked to Sebastian," I said, and Emma looked at me hopefully. "He has a girlfriend back in Puerto Rico. Or had. I'm not sure, but he seems pretty hung up on her still."

Emma nodded. "Yeah, that makes sense. Well, thanks for asking."

"So you're okay?" I asked.

"Of course," Emma said. "It was just a stupid crush."

I was so relieved! Emma seemed to be taking the news really well. And now I didn't have to worry about Emma crushing on Sebastian and whether or not he liked her back.

I gave my bracelet a little jangle. Thursday was just a bump in the road. My good luck was back, and I had a feeling it was going to stay that way.

CHAPTER 11

Totally Crummy!

Mmm . . . maple!" Katie said, dipping a tiny spoon into the frosting and tasting it. "This is definitely maple-y enough now."

Emma, Alexis, and I all took a taste.

"Definitely maple-y," Emma agreed.

It was Wednesday night, and we were in Katie's kitchen, baking cupcakes for the historical society event on Thursday. We do our baking at Katie's house a lot because her kitchen is stocked like a professional bakery—or, at least, it seems that way to me. There's a big pantry with five different kinds of flour (white flour, bread flour, wheat flour . . .), even more different kinds of sugar (white sugar, brown sugar, sparkling sugar . . .), jars of sprinkles in every color, and tons of baking pans and supplies.

Katie's kitchen is cheerful, too. It's white and yellow, and there are cute accessories on the counter, like a cookie jar with a smiley face on it. Colorful vintage aprons hang from hooks on the pantry door. It looks exactly like the kind of kitchen where cupcakes should be baked. Sometimes I think our cupcakes come out better when we bake them in Katie's kitchen.

"I made a test batch on my own over the weekend," Katie said. "I used pure maple syrup, but they didn't taste quite maple-y enough. So I looked up some recipes online, and a lot of them called for maple extract. It has a more concentrated flavor. Luckily, I found it at the supply shop."

"Don't forget to give me your receipt for that," Alexis said.

Katie nodded. "Yes, I saved it. You have trained me well."

Alexis grinned. "Finally!"

We had baked one sheet cake of chocolate cake, so that we could make the spools of thread, along with four dozen maple cupcakes with maple frosting, for the event. We had two left over, so when they were baked and frosted, we cut them in half and tasted them.

"Delicious!" Alexis said. "And they'll look

even more beautiful tomorrow when they're all decorated."

"I've got all the stuff," I said. "Tomorrow after school at my house."

"My dad can drive us to the society," Alexis explained. "He'll pick us up at four forty-five, so we'll have to decorate pretty quickly."

"That's almost two hours. We can do it," I said confidently.

Then we packed our finished cupcakes in the plastic carriers we have—to keep them fresh and from getting smooshed—and we called it a night.

The next day, after school, Katie took the bus all the way to my house. Emma and Alexis would have to get a ride since they live close to the school and aren't allowed to get on the bus with us. They would bring the cupcakes with them.

When Katie and I walked into the house, Mom and Eddie were standing in the living room, like they had been waiting for me.

"Hi, Katie!" Mom said. "I didn't know you were coming over today."

"We're decorating the cupcakes for the historical society event tonight," I said. "I told you."

Mom shook her head. "I don't think so," she

said. "Are you starting soon? Eddie and I need to talk to you."

She said it in that *You are in so much trouble* voice that she has. I got a bad feeling. I looked over at Katie, who was staring down at her sneakers.

"Katie, will you please excuse us while we talk in the kitchen?" Eddie asked.

"Sure," Katie said.

I followed Mom and Eddie into the kitchen. Mom launched in right away.

"Mia, I got an e-mail from Mrs. Kratzer, your social studies teacher," she said, and my heart sank. I definitely was in so much trouble. "You got a D+ on your last two quizzes, apparently, and your average has dropped from an A to a C-. She is worried about you. What's been going on?"

The doorbell rang. "I can't talk about it now," I said. "But it's no big deal. I didn't do the reading, but now I'm caught up."

"That is a big deal," Mom said sternly, and Eddie nodded behind her. "But I won't embarrass you in front of your friends. We'll discuss this later."

I was relieved, even though I knew I was probably in for it later. Katie had let in Emma and Alexis, and they marched into the kitchen with the cupcakes.

"I'll set up everything," I said, and from a cabinet, I got the supplies that Mom and I had purchased.

"Somebody needs to start cutting out the spool shapes," I said, putting the tube-shape cutter on the table. "And somebody else can turn the licorice into tiny balls of yarn."

"Ooh, me!" cried Emma, taking the bag of licorice from me.

"I'll start coloring and rolling out the fondant, and then we can stamp and cut out the button shapes," I said, and then I realized something. "Oh no! I forgot to buy the cute buttons!"

"Maybe your Mom has some," Alexis suggested. "Go ask her, and we'll get started here."

I found Mom in her office.

"Mom, do you have any buttons we could use?" I asked.

Mom looked confused. "I thought all your decorations had to be edible," she said.

"They do, but we need to stamp the buttons into the fondant to make the decorations," I said.

"What kind do you need?" Mom asked.

I showed her the one on my bracelet. "Cute ones, like this."

Mom frowned. "I think everything I've got is modern and kind of plain," she said. "But I'll get them in case there's something you can use."

I sighed. "Thanks, Mom."

When I got back to the kitchen, Alexis was mixing yellow coloring into the fondant, Emma was busy making yarn balls, and Katie had cut a dozen spool shapes out of the sheet cake.

"So how do I stick the cookies to the top and bottom of the spool of thread?" Katie asked. "With frosting, right?"

"Yeah," I replied, and then it hit me again. "Oh no! We forgot to make extra frosting!"

Alexis checked the clock. "Argh. Is there time?"

"I can make frosting in a flash. I'll run home to get some supplies, but I'll be right back," Katie said, rushing off to her house.

I felt terrible! It was my job to make sure everything was set for the decorations, and now we were scrambling. I remembered Katie's words.

Sometimes that's how the cupcake crumbles. I quickly banished the thought from my mind. The last thing we needed now was crumbling cupcakes!

Mom came into the kitchen with some plastic containers of buttons, and I quickly looked through them. She was right. They were mostly boring, but I found some small round ones with a raised border around the edge that would make good stamps.

They would work just fine, although they weren't as special as I had wanted. I looked down at my bracelet.

"Okay, lucky button, you're on," I said, and I detached it from the bracelet. Then I walked over to Alexis.

"I'll roll out the fondant," I said. "Can you make a batch of green and a batch of blue?"

Alexis nodded. "On it."

My hands were getting sweaty because I knew we were behind. I rolled out the fondant to about half an inch thick—it was okay if the buttons were a little thick, because they would hold up better.

Katie came back with frosting supplies and started on a new batch, and just when I was feeling like I had things under control, a sound like a truck crashing suddenly came from the basement.

"Oh, great. Band practice," Alexis said.

"Sorry, I forgot," I said.

"Katie, are you finished with that frosting?" Alexis asked. "I need to put some in my ears!"

"Well, I don't mind it," Emma said, and then there was kind of an awkwardness, because I guess we all knew about Sebastian's girlfriend by then. But the awkwardness disappeared because we were too busy to be awkward!

Emma rolled the thin licorice rope into a dozen adorable tiny balls of yarn. Then she helped Katie with the spools of thread. Each one was very painstaking. Katie finished the frosting (vanilla with blue food coloring) and filled up two pastry bags. One had a wide tip, and the other had a skinny tip. Katie used the wide tip to put a blob of frosting on one side of each cookie. Then she stuck a cookie onto each end of the spool-shaped chocolate cake.

Katie handed each spool off to Emma, and Emma used the pastry bag with the small tip to pipe a line of frosting around and around the spool, so that it looked like thread. The tip of her tongue stuck out of the corner of the mouth as she worked, concentrating.

"This is hard," she said.

"I'm sorry I can't help you," I said. "These buttons are taking forever!"

Alexis and I were stamping the buttons facedown into the fondant. Then we had to use a craft knife to cut around the buttons and gently lift them up out of the fondant. The first one I did broke—and for each cupcake, we needed four or five buttons for the best effect.

After I had made about twenty buttons, I looked at the clock. It was four fifteen, and I knew Alexis's dad, Mr. Becker, would be here in about a half an hour. Katie and Emma only had about five spools done, and none of the cupcakes had decorations on top yet!

While I was worrying, the music stopped, and the sound of stomping came up the stairs. Dan, Sebastian, and the two other guys in the band came up. This time, instead of going their separate ways, they all came into the kitchen.

"It's the Cupcake Club!" said Sebastian, grinning.

"Dan, we're really busy right now," I said. "Do you mind?"

The two other guys were leaning over the table, curious. Alexis eyed them.

"Hey, do you guys want to help?" she asked.

They shrugged.

"Sure," said one kid. "What do you need?"

Dan was leaning against the refrigerator with a glass of milk, rolling his eyes.

"Wash your hands," she instructed, and to my amazement, the boys obeyed.

"Who's the lead guitarist?" she asked, and a boy with a crew cut raised his hand.

"Me. I'm Mark."

"Okay, Mark, you've got dexterity in your

fingers. See if you can help Emma with the spools of thread. Sebastian, help Katie with the cookies. Other guy, we need you to put four buttons on each cupcake. Choose different colors and make them look nice," Alexis ordered. "Dan, you can do that too."

I watched, amazed, as the boys went to work. They didn't seem to mind taking orders from an eighth-grade girl—but Alexis is not your average eighth-grade girl.

I was even more amazed when the boys ended up doing a great job. Sam was great with the frosting, and he made the spools of thread look exactly like small, edible spools of thread! Emma began to place the finished ones on the cupcakes.

When Alexis and I finally stopped cutting out buttons, Dan and the other guy (whose name, I later found out, was Rick) helped us put the buttons on the rest of the cupcakes. Then we all pitched in, carefully putting the cupcakes back into their holders just as we heard a car's horn beep outside.

"My dad's here!" Alexis announced, heading for the door.

"Okay, we just need to wash up," I said. I turned to Dan. "Thanks."

Dan shrugged. "No problem."

Katie washed her hands in the sink and was drying them on a towel when Sebastian walked up to her.

"Hey, Katie, maybe we can get a pizza sometime," he said.

Emma was at the sink too, and she shut off the water. The kitchen got quiet really fast.

Katie looked confused. "You mean, you and me? Just the two of us?"

"Yeah," said Sebastian. "I thought we could hang out."

"Thanks, but I kind of have a boyfriend, sort of," Katie babbled awkwardly. "I mean, I'm not allowed to have a boyfriend yet, but if I did have one, it would be George. George Martinez. He's in my grade."

Sebastian smiled. "Oh, okay," he said.

What was that all about? I wondered, but then Sebastian walked up to me.

"I thought you said she liked me?" he asked in a loud whisper.

"I never said that!" I protested, and then, from the corner of my eye, I saw Emma listening to us. She ran out of the house, and I ran after her.

I'm fast, but Emma was faster. She darted around the corner before I could catch up to her. Alexis walked up to me, holding two cupcake carriers.

"What was that about?" she asked.

"It's a big mess," I explained. "For some stupid reason, Sebastian thought I told him that Katie liked him. I just said one of my friends liked him, and he thought it was Katie because of the way she jokes around with him. And now Emma's mad at me."

Alexis looked down the empty street. "She's probably just embarrassed. I'll text her on the way to the historical society. We really need to get those cupcakes there on time."

"This is awful," I said. "I'm so sorry."

Katie came out with the rest of the cupcake holders, looking upset. "Where did that come from?" she asked. "Why does Sebastian think I like him? And where's Emma?"

"It's a long story." I sighed. "Come on, we'd better go."

We loaded up the car, and Alexis's dad drove us to the historical society. The whole way there, I looked out the window, hoping to see Emma. I felt terrible.

This was more than just crumbling cupcakes. This was bad luck, for sure!

CHAPTER 12

I Finally Figure It Out!

It felt weird going to the historical society without Emma. The society is in an old Victorian home on a street lined with maple trees. Mr. Becker helped us carry the cupcake stands we use into the building.

When we got inside, Sophie and her mom were there to greet us. Mrs. Baudin was all dressed up in a chic black suit, her hair pulled back in a low bun.

"The cupcakes are here!" she cried happily. "Sophie, help the girls set things up. I can't wait to see them!"

"Sure," Sophie said. "Dessert's going to be held in the parlor."

She led us into a room at the front of the house.

The furniture all looked like something out of the past. There was a pretty sofa against the wall, upholstered in pink fabric with cream flowers, set in a frame of dark wood that was carved with more flowers. On the opposite wall was a carved wooden table with a white tablecloth draped over it, flanked by two chairs that matched the couch. A modern-day folding table with a cloth over it had been set up for the cupcakes.

What interested me most, though, were the blown-up black-and-white photographs set up on easels around the room. They showed rows and rows of women bent over sewing machines, hard at work.

I studied one of the photos. "Wow," I said. "Can you imagine doing that all day?"

"And it was a long day," said Mrs. Baudin, coming up behind me. "Twelve, thirteen, fourteen hours sometimes."

I shook my head. "That's hard to believe."

"I'll take the cupcake business over that any day," said Katie as she carefully placed the cupcakes onto the cupcake stands we had brought.

Mrs. Baudin clapped her hands and went to the table. "Oh my goodness, look how perfect these are! Yarn! Thread! Buttons!"

"And they're maple flavored, for Maple Grove," Katie added.

"Wonderful!" said Mrs. Baudin. "Now, which one of you gets the check?"

"That would be me," said Alexis, handing her a business card in return. "Thank you for your business. Please recommend us to your friends."

"Oh, I will," Mrs. Baudin said. "In fact, if you have some more cards on you, I'll distribute them to the members of the society."

Alexis grinned. "Of course I have more cards!" she said. "Thank you. We appreciate that."

I studied the photos a little bit more as we packed up our carriers.

"These will be on display all month," Mrs. Baudin told me. "You should come back some other time."

"Thanks, I would like that," I said, and I meant it. Something about those photos was really getting to me. But I couldn't put my finger on it, because I was still worried about Emma.

"Did she text you back?" I asked Alexis when we got in the car.

"She's home," Alexis replied. "She doesn't feel like talking. But I'm sure she'll be fine by tomorrow. I tried to explain to her what happened."

"Thanks," I said, and I leaned back against the car seat. I felt exhausted.

When I got home, Sebastian and the band guys were gone and Eddie had dinner on the stove—his famous spaghetti. After dinner, I realized I had a vocab sheet to do, and I sighed. I spread out the contents of my backpack in the dining room and looked at the clock. It was seven o'clock.

Twelve, thirteen, fourteen hours, Mrs. Baudin had said. So if those women had started early in the morning, they might still be sewing. What a long, hard day they had had.

Even my unluckiest day is not that bad, I realized, and that felt like a big, important thing to realize. But you know how it is with big, important things—one minute, they're important, and the next minute, you forget all about them.

That's kind of what happened over the next few days. It started right after I finished my homework that Thursday night, when Mom and Eddie sat across the table from me.

"About your grade in social studies," Mom began, and I braced myself for what was coming.

"It seems like your issue is that you need to focus on schoolwork, Mia," Mom continued. "So Eddie, your dad, and I have agreed that you can

119

do with a break from electronics for a few days. Starting tonight. Your privileges resume Monday morning."

"No electronics?" I asked, panic rising in my voice. "Like what, exactly?"

"As in no phone, no television, no computer," Mom said. "Unless you need your computer for homework."

How unfair was that? "All weekend? Are you kidding me?" I wailed.

"Mrs. Kratzer is giving you an extra-credit project to bring up your grade, so I'm sure you'll have plenty to do to keep you busy," Mom said in that annoyingly calm voice of hers.

I knew there was no point in arguing when her voice is like that, so I stuffed my books into my backpack and stomped upstairs as loudly as I could. Then I slammed the door shut behind me.

The thing is, part of me knew Mom was right. But part of me felt like the punishment was unfair. I had already caught up to the reading. What more did she want?

Mom hadn't said anything about *Teen Runway*, so I read it again from cover to cover until I fell asleep.

It was raining again the next morning—and for

the next three days. That was just as well, because it fit my mood.

On Friday, I tried to apologize to Emma at lunch.

"Sebastian totally misunderstood me," I said. "I told him one of my friends liked him, and then when he said he had a girlfriend, I figured it didn't matter, so I didn't tell him it was you."

"I don't really want to talk about it," Emma said, picking at her salad with a fork. "It doesn't matter what you said to him. He asked out Katie, so he can't be that hung up on his girlfriend. And he doesn't like me, anyway. So let's all forget about it, okay?"

Neither of us said another word, and lunch was pretty quiet after that. Then I had to go to Mrs. Kratzer's class, where she approached me before the bell rang.

"Mia, I have something for you," she said, handing me an envelope.

"Thanks," I mumbled, and took it back to my seat. Inside was a sheet that read:

Extra-Credit Project: Do a report on fashion during China's Han dynasty. What did nobles wear? Officials?

Common people? Children? Your report should include ten different examples accompanied by art. Sketches are welcome.

I noticed that Mrs. Kratzer was looking at me expectantly; she probably thought she was doing me a favor by giving me a fashion project. But I was still in a bad mood about being punished, so I didn't give her the satisfaction of smiling at her or anything.

After school, Mom drove me to the train station. She handed my phone back to me before I got out of the car.

"This is for the train ride only, in case you need to communicate with me or your dad," she said. "He'll take it from you when you get there."

"Yeah, great," I said.

Mom leaned over and kissed me. "Bye, Mia. Love you." And I kissed her back, because I love her too, even when I think she is being totally unfair.

The train ride was boring, but I listened to music on my phone and tried to sketch in my sketchbook. The rain beat down on the windows, so I drew a long dress with layers and layers of fringe that looked like rain, rain, rain . . .

Dad showed up at the train station with a string of bad news. "Tokyo 16 is closed for a private party, so I thought we'd just grab some pizza," he said. "And I have to work tomorrow, even though I tried really hard to get out of it. Oh, and your mom says I need to take your phone."

"Yeah, I know," I said, handing it over.

And so began a long, boring weekend. Well, mostly boring. I tried to get together with Ava, but she was visiting her grandmother for the weekend. Then I told Dad I needed to use my laptop for my extra credit, and when he left for his meeting or whatever, I turned it on. I figured I'd watch a video or something and then work on my report later.

You really don't want to mess this up again, warned Practical Mia, and I knew she was right. So I typed in "Han Dynasty Fashion."

To my surprise, the images that came up were of these really beautiful outfits, and flowing skirts with jackets, all in gorgeous colors. I was hooked. I was still sketching when Dad came back from work.

"What do you say, Mia?" Dad asked. "Chinese food and we rent a movie?"

"Uh, no electronics, remember? It's part of my punishment," I reminded him.

123

Dad frowned. "Well, did you do all your homework?" he asked.

"Yes," I replied. "And I'm almost done with my extra credit."

"Well, why don't you finish up, and we'll see," he said. "I mean, watching a movie with me is quality family time. I don't think that should count."

"Me either," I said, grinning. And what Mom didn't know wouldn't hurt her.

But the movie ended up being boring, anyway, and it was still raining the next day when Dad brought me to the train. I hugged him good-bye and then spent another long, dreary train ride back to Maple Grove.

When I got off the train, I tucked my phone into the front pocket of my backpack. Then I hurried over to Mom's car and climbed in.

"How was your weekend?" she asked.

"Boring," I snapped.

"Laura and Sebastian are over," she said.

"That's nice," I replied, not wanting to give her the satisfaction of a conversation.

We spent the rest of the trip in silence. Then, when we got home, I stepped out of the car—and my phone slipped out of my backpack and into a big puddle! I had forgotten to zip the pocket closed.

"Nooooo!" I wailed, fishing it out of the puddle.

"Oh boy," Mom said. "Let's hurry inside and try to dry that out."

Mom took the phone from me, and we went inside. Laura surprised me with a hug.

"Mia, how good to see you!" she said. "Thanks for keeping Sebastian company while I've been so busy."

"Don't thank me, thank Dan," I said.

Then Laura looked at my wrist and smiled. "You're wearing the bracelet! I'm so glad."

"It's nice," I told her. "But I don't think it brings good luck."

Then, like a sudden storm, I started to cry like a baby. I don't know where it came from, but I couldn't stop it.

"Mia, what's wrong?" Laura asked, leading me over to the couch.

"Everything!" I groaned. "Everything that can go wrong is going wrong. Emma is hurt because of me, because I made Sebastian think that Katie likes him instead of her. I messed up in social studies. I almost messed up our cupcake order. I keep dropping things! I am cursed!"

Mom came over and sat next to me. I had her on one side, and Laura on the other.

"Oh, honey," Mom said. "You're not cursed. There's good luck, and there's bad luck sometimes, sure. But mostly I think we make our own luck."

My tears were drying out. "What do you mean?"

"Well, there are things you can do that will usually get you good results. For example, if you study, then it helps you pass a test," Mom said. "If you wake up early, then you won't be late."

"But what if the power goes off and your alarm clock doesn't wake you up?" I asked.

"Then that's bad luck—something that you can't control," Mom said. "But there are plenty of other things that we can control."

I nodded, and another big realization was hitting me. Some of those things that happened were bad luck. And some were just my fault. If I wanted to, I could turn things around. Make my own luck.

"Sometimes we make our own luck," I repeated. "I like that."

Then Laura grabbed my wrist. "And, Mia, the *azabache* is more than just a good luck charm," she said. "It is a symbol of the love that a family has for the child who gets it. You don't need luck when you are loved."

Then she hugged me again, and this time I got

126

it—not just in my head, but deep inside, where it counts.

"I like that too," I said. "And I'll keep wearing the bracelet. And not for luck—but to remember what an awesome family I have."

Now, Mom hugged me. "That's my girl."

And suddenly, squashed between my mom and my cousin, I felt really happy. Which was weird when just a few minutes ago I had been sobbing.

Then I noticed Sebastian was hovering near us.

"Sorry to interrupt this love fiesta," he said. "But did you say that Emma likes me? The cute preppy blonde?"

"Of course," I said. "Couldn't you tell? She likes the music you play, and she talked to you about it every time she saw you."

Sebastian smiled, and I would have to describe it as a mysterious smile. Was he intrigued? I wasn't going to ask. If Sebastian liked Emma, it was up to him to tell her.

That night, I slept like a baby—but not before I finished my extra credit project, read ahead one chapter in social studies, and made sure I set my alarm. Because from now on, I'm making my own luck!

Want another sweet cupcake?
Here's a sneak peek
of the next book in the
CUPCAKE  DIARIES
series:

Emma
raining cats
and dogs...and
cupcakes!

Arf!

I am a major dog-lover, but even the barking was getting to me! Twenty happy dogs in all shapes and sizes were excited and running around the grassy yard, playing with balls and ropes and jumping in and out of a doggy play structure in the center of the action.

Mrs. Barnett, the petite, blond director of ARF (Animal Rescue Fund), laughed and called above the din, "Why don't you girls come back to my office so we can hear ourselves think?"

The Cupcakers and I all laughed in agreement, and we followed her out of the fenced-in play yard and back down the tiled hall.

We, the Cupcake Club—me (Emma Taylor) and my best friends and business partners, Alexis Becker, Mia Vélaz-Cruz, and Katie Brown—were at our local pet shelter for a meeting about some cupcakes we would be baking for an event they were having. The four of us have a business baking cupcakes for special events for friends, family, and clients (who often become like friends and family). We've done everything from kids' parties to movie premieres, celebrity weddings to moms' book clubs. We are creative and our cupcakes are reasonably priced, and we deliver! Our motto is: Professional cupcakes with a homemade twist.

Today we'd been recommended to ARF by a boy from our school who volunteers there—Diego Diaz. Diego is always Instagramming things about pets that need homes, and events being held at the shelter. He's really into helping animals and has raised a lot of awareness about abandoned animals, as well as helping to raise money for ARF. Now, ARF is having an adopt-a-pet event next weekend at our local park, and Diego suggested they hand out cupcakes to entice passersby to stop and mingle with the cats and dogs they'll have on-site for adoption. Mrs. Barnett loved the idea, so she'd contacted us and asked us to come in for a tour and meeting.

We settled into her cramped office—Alexis on an extra chair, taking notes on her laptop, Mia and

Katie perched on a windowsill, and me leaning in the doorway—and chatted about what kind of turnout ARF could expect for the park event and what they hoped to gain from it.

Mrs. Barnett explained, "Usually, we bring four kittens, two cats, at least two or three puppies, and then two older dogs. We expect to have about seventy people stop by the table during our three hours in the park. So maybe let's order . . . five dozen cupcakes, since I don't think everyone will take one. How does that sound?"

Alexis was nodding as she jotted it all down. "Great. So it's next Saturday. And we'll meet you at eleven, in the park, right? It's easier than you having to transport the cupcakes if we bring them there first."

"Yes. Thanks," agreed Mrs. Barnett.

We exchanged cell numbers.

"We'll come up with a design proposal for you to approve before this weekend," Alexis said, and continued to outline the terms, but all I could think about were the poor animals that needed homes. Cupcakes were far from my mind.

"Um, excuse me, Mrs. Barnett? How many of the animals do you usually place at an event like this?" I had to know.

Mrs. Barnett smiled. "The kittens are the easiest. We'll almost always place a kitten. About once every three or four months, we'll place a puppy. Maybe once a year we place an older dog this way. But we do yield about five on-site visits from these events. . . ."

I must have looked confused, because she looked at me kindly and explained.

"People follow up with a visit here to the shelter. And those tend to be more productive for us than the park events, because, of course, if people are bothering to come see us, they are usually pretty ready to adopt."

I felt my chest relax a little. "Oh. Good. I just can't stand to think of all those poor animals . . ." I wasn't sure how to finish my sentence.

Mrs. Barnett nodded sympathetically. "I know. We are a no-kill shelter, though. We won't put down animals just because we can't find homes for them. Every once in a while there's a really difficult animal who we have to refer elsewhere—severe biters, feral cats, attack dogs, what have you—but we do eventually find someplace for everyone. It can sometimes take more than a year."

"Poor little guys," I said.

She nodded again, then she said briskly, "But

our pity really doesn't help them. People need to have their animals spayed and neutered, so they don't reproduce, and we need to keep the profile of ARF in the public eye so people continue to donate to us. That's where your cupcakes come in!" She stood up to signal that our meeting was over. Alexis closed her laptop and stood to shake Mrs. Barnett's hand.

"Thanks so much for the opportunity to bake for you," said Alexis. "We're sure you'll love the results!"

Mrs. Barnett laughed and patted her stomach. "That's what I'm worried about!"

We laughed with her, and my stress eased a bit. Alexis was always so professional, and it kept things flowing. We were quickly outside and ready to call for our ride. Even from the sidewalk, though, the barking was pretty crazy.

"Those poor doggies," I said.

Katie looped her arm across my shoulders and gave me a squeeze. "I know. I could tell you were taking it hard, you little animal lover, you."

"I'm going to give Tiki and Milkshake extra doggy treats when I get home today," said Mia. She shook her head as if to clear her mind. "It's so sad that people just ditch their pets like that. I can't even imagine it. It just breaks my heart."

"Pets are expensive," Alexis said briskly. "It would be sadder if they ditched their kids when times got tough."

"Alexis!" I reprimanded her.

She shrugged. "Sorry, but it's true. I'm stunned by how much money is spent on pets in this country."

"All right, boss lady! We don't need an economics lesson!" teased Mia.

Alexis sniffed. "I might just have to go into the pet-supply business when I get older."

We giggled, and pretty soon after, my dad rolled up in our minivan and we piled in.

"How did it go?" he asked as the door slid shut behind us.

"Oh, Dad, it was so sad!" I wailed, buckling my seat belt. "There are so many animals that need homes!"

He nodded. "I can't even go into those places. I'd come out with enough pets to fill an ark!"

"Maybe we should!" I said enthusiastically.

But he smiled and shook his head. "I don't deny that we are getting closer to convincing your mom to get a dog. *But there is still much work for us to do . . . ,*" he said in a fake formal tone.

My three brothers and I have wanted a dog for years, ever since our old Lab, Sissy, died. My youngest brother, Jake, in particular, is dying for a dog of his own. Since he's pretty spoiled, he'll probably get it. I'm just hoping he'll be willing to share.

I've always loved dogs—I like cats, too, but not in the same way—and snuggling with Sissy is one of my earliest memories. Her warm, soft fur; her silky ears that she'd let me play with whenever I wanted; her strong, quiet heartbeat when I laid my head on her and used her as a TV pillow; that coziness that always made me feel happy. I loved how safe she made me feel and how she was always overjoyed to see me. It was the best feeling.

For the past few years I've been earning extra money by walking dogs in the neighborhood. I used to have a bigger business, but it got overwhelming and I had to dial it back. It is pretty incredible how many pets are out there and how much money can be made from them. But as much as I love other people's pets, there's nothing quite like having one of your own. More importantly, I just don't like to see animals suffer.

"It's just so sad, all those animals in there—"

Alexis interrupted me. "Wait. It would be sad if they were all boxed in, in cages and whatever.

But it's *not* sad, because ARF has those play yards for the dogs, and that indoor playroom for the cats, and all the volunteers, and good food. . . . It's pricey but worth it. Kind of like boarding school for pets. Think of it that way!" Then she frowned. "Hmm. Maybe that's an idea for my Future Business Leaders project." She whipped out her phone and began making notes, her fingers flying.

I laughed and shook my head. Alexis is so practical and driven.

"Listen, what are we thinking to bake for them?" asked Katie. "I have loads of cute ideas on my computer that could be good. We could do little sugar cookies cut in the shape of dog bones on top of chocolate frosting. . . ."

"Cute," agreed Mia. "Or paw prints?"

Katie nodded. "Or I have some more elaborate designs we could try. . . ."

I agreed. "I'm up for anything. I think Mrs. Barnett is too. Lex?"

"Hmmm?" She was texting away madly.

"I had a thought. . . ."

Mia and Katie looked at me as we turned onto Katie's street.

"Lex?" I asked again quietly.

She looked up at me.

"What if we didn't charge?"

Alexis blinked, not comprehending. "What?" she said finally.

I glanced at the other two Cupcakers. They understood what I was getting at. Mia's eyebrows were raised in surprise, but a smile was forming on Katie's face.

"What if we made the cupcakes a donation?" I pressed.

Alexis sighed a huge sigh. I could see her running the numbers in her head. . . . Well, sixty cupcakes . . . and at a unit cost of seventy-five cents per . . . plus transport time . . .

"Just think about it, okay?" I asked.

Mia and Katie nodded from the back row.

"Okay. I'll think about it. I just don't want to set a bad precedent. Lots of our clients are nonprofits," said Alexis.

"I know. But those poor doggies. . . ."

"We've never done that before," continued Alexis. "Not charged."

"What about a deep discount?" offered Mia.

Alexis started to nod.

"Don't decide now, Lex. You look into it, and we'll discuss it at the weekly meeting on Wednesday, okay?" I felt good, though. I could tell

I was going to win this one. I smiled to myself.

"By the way," added Katie, "we should do something as a thank-you to Diego Diaz for the referral, don't you think?"

"Good call!" I agreed heartily. A smile spread across my face, and I could feel a blush coming on. Katie looked at me, and I am sure she noticed my reaction to hearing Diego's name, but she was kind enough to not say anything.

"Yeah. Maybe let's bake a few extra for him, and we can drop them off. Emma can drop them off," Mia teased. So now I was really blushing. I gestured to my dad driving, and they got my drift and quieted down quickly, thank goodness.

We pulled into Katie's driveway, which was a welcome distraction from the topic at hand.

"Okay, Katie! Hope to see you soon!" joked my dad. My friends come over all the time.

"Thanks, Mr. Taylor," she said, sliding open the door and hopping out onto the blacktop.

"So four o'clock at the movies?" she asked.

We agreed. We'd meet after we finished our weekend homework, and then we'd see the new Liam Carey movie and have a quick bite at the mall.

Our next stop was Mia's, and of course, what I was dreading most, happened. Her cousin Sebastian, who I thought was really cute when he moved here a while ago, was hanging out with her step-brother, Dan, on the front stoop. I'd had a crush on Sebastian, but things got all mixed up and he asked out Katie, and now I just really never want to see him again. Even if he is still pretty cute.

Mia saw them and glanced quickly at me. "Thanks, Mr. Taylor. I can get out right here. . . ." We were still a house away, and my dad was obviously aiming to pull into her driveway. Then there'd be no avoiding Sebastian.

"Oh, it's no problem," said my dad.

"Dad," I said sharply. "Please don't pull in." I sank low in my seat in hopes the boys wouldn't see me through the tinted window.

He gave me a weird look in the rearview mirror, but luckily, he did as we asked. Mia slid open the door on the street side so she wouldn't have to climb over me.

"Careful, honey!" said my dad as a car inched by on that side.

I squeezed Mia's hand before she left. She knew I was thanking her for her consideration in not exposing me to Sebastian again. She squeezed back.

"Thanks, Mr. Taylor. See you girls at the mall!"

She hopped out and pushed the close button on the door so fast, it nearly caught her as she exited. "Oops!" She laughed.

My dad was shaking his head. "You girls are going to be the death of me," he said. "Always some kind of mystery agenda going on . . ." He eased his way back onto the road and continued until we dropped off Alexis.

As we drove home from her house, I could feel my dad checking on me in the rearview mirror again. "Everything okay, lovebug?" he asked.

I nodded and looked out the window. The Sebastian and Katie thing had been embarrassing, and I was only just feeling like I was over it, but now it was all back again. I was new to the whole boy thing, and I wasn't sure I liked this kind of drama.

"Who's Diego?" Dad asked with a smile.

Oh, well, Diego was another story. Not much of a story, actually. Yet. Maybe. A smiled bloomed on my face, anyway. "A guy in Matt's class at school."

My dad smiled again at me, clearly waiting for more. But I just continued to look out the window. There truly *wasn't* any more to say right now. So after a pause, during which my dad realized he wasn't getting any info out of me, he reached over and turned up the radio, which was playing some dorky eighties song from his youth. Then he bopped his head and patted the steering wheel in time to the beat for the final part of our trip home. It was majorly embarrassing.

Want more

CUPCAKE🧁DIARIES?

Visit **CupcakeDiariesBooks.com**
for the series trailer, excerpts, activities,
and everything you need for throwing
your own cupcake party!

Still Hungry?
There's always room for another Cupcake!

If you liked

CUPCAKE  DIARIES

be sure to check out these

other series from

Simon Spotlight

sewzoey

Zoey's clothing design blog puts her on the A-list in the fashion world . . . but when it comes to school, will she be teased, or will she be a trendsetter? Find out in the Sew Zoey series:

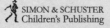

Coco Simon always dreamed of opening a cupcake bakery but was afraid she would eat all of the profits. When she's not daydreaming about cupcakes, Coco edits children's books and has written close to one hundred books for children, tweens, and young adults, which is a lot less than the number of cupcakes she's eaten. Cupcake Diaries is the first time Coco has mixed her love of cupcakes with writing.